BREAKING UP IS REALLY, REALLY HARD TO DO

a **DATING GAME** novel by Natalie Standiford

LITTLE, BROWN AND COMPANY

New York ⋏ Boston

First Edition: June 2005

Little, Brown and Company
Time Warner Book Group
1271 Avenue of the Americas, New York, NY 10020
Visit our Web site at www.lb-teens.com

Interior created and produced by Parachute Publishing, L.L.C.
156 Fifth Avenue
New York, NY 10010

ISBN: 0-316-11041-8

10 9 8 7 6 5 4 3 2 1

CWO

For Nancy Williams

1 Phony Baloney

HERE IS TODAY'S HOROSCOPE: CAPRICORN: Everything you
want is right under your nose—but yours is stuck up so high
in the air you can't see it. Try coming down to earth a bit . . .
a little lower . . . little lower . . . You're going to have to do
better than that.

It started with a shirt—a neon orange t-shirt. The
color on its own was bad enough, although Rob
Safran, with his warm olive skin and brown eyes,
pulled it off better than Holly Anderson had any right to
expect. That wasn't the problem. The problem was what
was printed on the shirt.

You Say "Psycho" Like It's A Bad Thing

"I'm sorry," Holly said. "It's not funny."

"It's just a t-shirt," Rob said. "It's a joke."

"Yeah, well . . . if you ever had a psychopath in your family, you'd be more sensitive about it," Holly said.

Rob looked stricken. "I'm sorry—do you have a psychopath in your family?"

"Well, no, not that I know of," Holly said. "But there are days when my mother comes close."

Rob laughed, but Holly was serious. About the t-shirt, anyway. Rob's family gave each other tasteless t-shirts for every birthday and holiday in an ongoing contest to see who could out-cheese the others. Rob seemed to have one for every day of the year. I'm with Stupid, I'm So Poor I Can't Pay Attention, Virginia Is for Lovers, Ithaca Is Gorges . . .

Sometimes I can't believe he's my boyfriend, Holly thought, and she meant it in both the good way and the bad way. There were days when she looked at his strong swimmer's build, high cheekbones and messy brown hair and thought, *He's like a buff teddy bear. I'm the luckiest girl in Carlton Bay!*

And there were other days when she could always find something annoying about him. When she wondered if she couldn't find someone better. When she thought, *I can't look at one more corny t-shirt.*

But the thing that bothered Holly the most about Rob was when he asked permission to kiss her. *If I hear "Mind if I kiss you?" one more time, I'll scream,* she thought.

Today was looking like one of those days. Holly stretched out on the sunroom couch, pressing her feet into Rob's side. Rob had stopped by her house just to hang out on a Saturday afternoon, no plans. Holly's parents had gone antiquing somewhere or other. They loved to look at antiques, which Holly found strange, since they rarely bought them. The Andersons' house was spacious and contemporary, and most of the furniture was new.

Holly twisted her long, wavy blond hair and pinned it on top of her head. Rob took her feet in his lap and playfully pinched her toes.

"Let's do something," he said. "Want to do something?"

"Sure," Holly said. "What do you want to do?"

"I don't know," Rob said. "Whatever you want to do."

Holly tried to think of something fun to do. "We could go eat somewhere, I guess."

Rob rubbed her feet. "Yeah. Let's get some lunch. If that's what you want."

"Okay," she said. "What do you want to eat?"

He shrugged. "I don't know. Whatever you want."

She sat up, pulling her feet off his lap. He could be so

wishy-washy sometimes! He never said what he wanted. He always waited for her to decide. Why couldn't he pick a place to eat just once?

"Anything I want?" she asked.

"Anything."

"Okay," she said. "I know just the place."

They got into her yellow VW Beetle—a sixteenth birthday present from her parents—and she drove him to a vegan café called Phony Baloney. Everything looked—and supposedly tasted—like meat but was really made of tofu, wheat gluten, tempeh, and other vegetable by-products. Holly wasn't a vegetarian, and neither was Rob. But Rob always wanted her to decide where they should eat, so she thought she'd play a little joke on him.

Rob gulped when he saw the sign. "This is where you want to eat?"

"Yep. Unless you'd rather go somewhere else." She waited, half-hoping he'd beg her to turn the car around and head for the nearest McDonald's.

"Me? No. It's cool," he said.

They ordered Sham Ham Sandwiches and organic apple juice. The Sham Ham tasted more like cardboard than meat. "Enjoying your sandwich?" Holly asked after she struggled to swallow another bite.

Rob nodded. "Mmm-hmm. I'm loving it."

Liar, she thought. But she was no better. "Isn't it great? I feel so healthy."

"Me, too. I could eat this every day."

Rob swallowed another bite of Sham Ham. Holly took a deep breath and tackled her sandwich again. She put the sandwich to her lips once more, then dropped it on her plate.

"I can't eat this crap anymore," she said.

His eyes widened. "You don't like it? But you wanted to come here."

"I know. It was a bad joke," Holly said.

He dropped his sandwich, too. "A joke? I don't get it."

"Let's get out of here."

Rob grinned. "Good. I could go for a burger."

"Me, too."

They left some money on the table. Rob stood up and grabbed her.

"Mind if I kiss you?"

"Check Rebecca," Holly said. "She's actually eating carbs."

Holly and her best friends, Madison Markowitz and Lina Ozu, sat at a picnic table outside the lunchroom Monday afternoon, watching Rebecca Hulse and David Kim feed each other spaghetti. Rebecca, a skinny blond alpha girl, was normally a bit of an ice princess, but David seemed to have melted her. She cooed and slurped up a forkful of noodles, tomato sauce splattering her chin.

"David has turned Rebecca to mush," Holly said.

"For a split second I thought she wasn't cool anymore," Mads said. "But then I realized—all she did was change the definition of cool. I'm suddenly desperate to grab a boy and start slapping spaghetti all over him."

Rebecca and David nibbled a long strand of pasta, each starting at one end until their lips met in the middle.

Holly had matched them up herself. She and Mads and Lina had started a Web site called The Dating Game for a school project. It was a survey of sexual attitudes among the students at their school, the Rosewood School for Alternative Gifted Education, or RSAGE. It included personal ads and a matchmaking questionnaire that was so popular the girls kept the site going even after they'd aced the project.

"David's cute," Holly said. "Why didn't I ever notice it before?"

"Because you have Rob," Mads said. "He blocked you from noticing other guys."

"Well, it's not working anymore," Holly said. She wondered if David had to ask permission every time he kissed a girl. And so far she'd never seen him wearing a t-shirt that said, GIVE BLOOD—PLAY HOCKEY.

"So Rob wears a dumb t-shirt once in a while, so what?" Lina said.

"I know," Holly said. "Something must be wrong with me. But I can't help it. I keep wondering if Rob is the perfect guy for me. You know—is he IT?"

"How do you know if a guy is 'it'?" Lina asked. "What's the definition?"

"You just feel it," Mads said.

"But what do you feel?" Holly asked.

"I don't know," Mads said. "You feel nervous around him."

"Your heart beats faster when you think about him," Lina said. "Your mouth goes dry when you try to talk to him."

"You get this weird queasy-happy feeling in your stomach and your head," Mads said.

"You mean you feel sick," Holly said.

"Definitely," Lina said.

"I don't feel any of those things around Rob," Holly said. "Not now, anyway."

Mads and Lina both had huge, unrequited crushes on guys who were almost impossible to get. Lina was in love with Dan Shulman, their Interpersonal Human Development teacher, and Mads had been crazy for Sean Benedetto, the hottest senior in school, since he first strutted across her field of vision. Holly knew they were thinking of Dan and Sean when they talked about "it." But that wasn't what Holly wanted. She didn't want to long for the impossible. She wanted the perfect fit.

"This would be a good topic for a quiz," Mads said. The Dating Game site also included quizzes on topics from "Are You a Geek?" to "Do You Know How to Decode the Personals?"

"Holly!" Autumn Nelson yelled from the lunchroom window. She ran outside, her glossy brunette braids flapping, and plopped herself beside Holly on the bench. "When are you guys going to fix me up with somebody? I filled out your Dating Game questionnaire weeks ago."

"Soon, Autumn," Holly said. "Sorry—we had kind of a backlog."

"Well, hurry up!" Autumn said. "Move me to the front of the list or something. Now that Trent's gone mental, I need a new guy."

"What do you mean, 'Trent's gone mental'?" Lina asked.

"Who's Trent?" Mads asked.

"Oh, this dork I was seeing." Autumn waved the question away. "He stopped calling me for some stupid reason. At first I thought maybe he was dead, but then I spotted him down at the marina. So I figured he was gay, but finally I realized he must have lost his mind. Because how could you turn away from someone like me?" She waved a hand over her body as if her fabulousness spoke for itself. "You'd have to be on glue or something, right? Anyway, forget about him. Find me a new boyfriend! I'm tired of waiting for you losers to get off your fat butts!" She turned and went inside.

Mads' jaw dropped. "Just for that, I don't feel like helping her."

"We have to," Holly said. "If we don't, she'll trash us online and nobody will trust us to match them up. The Dating Game will die a slow, painful death."

Autumn aired her every thought, feeling, and action on her blog, Nuclear Autumn. The whole school read it. It gave her a lot of power—no one could afford to cross Autumn, or they'd risk being trashed. And right now The Dating Game—and all the gossip, matches, and talk it created—was responsible for a good twenty percent rise in the popularity ratings of Holly, Lina, and Mads.

"What are we going to do?" Lina asked. "Nobody will want to date her. She's too self-centered."

Is that my problem, too? Holly wondered. *Or is Rob really not "it?" How can I tell?*

2 Deep vs. Dope

To:	mad4u
From:	your daily horoscope

HERE IS TODAY'S HOROSCOPE: VIRGO: You think you know what you want, Virgo, but you're wrong. Stop trying to think for yourself and listen to me for a change!

T here he goes," Mads said. "My muse." Her eyes trailed Sean Benedetto as he loped across the school courtyard. Mads sat with Holly and Lina on the grass during a free period on a warm Tuesday afternoon. Tall, athletic Sean, with his shaggy blond hair, was the love of Mads' life. And now, the inspiration for her art.

The annual RSAGE Art Fair was coming up and Mads

was planning a major project. She was going to draw pastel portraits of her friends, family, acquaintances, and maybe even pets, with a portrait of Sean as the centerpiece. He was so good-looking, how could she go wrong? Even a bad picture of him might win a prize.

"Am I going to be in your art project?" Lina asked.

"Definitely," Mads said. "And Holly, too. And guess what? My parents are letting me throw a party after the fair. An after-show celebration. And I can invite as many people as I want."

"Excellent," Holly said.

"The only thing is, there might be teachers there," Mads said. "My stupid parents thought it would be nice to invite some of them and make it like a school thing."

"That's okay," Holly said. "That way you know Lina will come for sure."

"Hey!" Lina tossed a pen at Holly.

"When can we see the ad?" Mads asked. Lina had found a personal ad Dan Shulman had posted on a dating Web site. Mads was dying to see it. Unlike Lina, she found it hard to picture Dan in a dating context.

"Come over tonight," Lina said. "You can help me figure out what to write to him."

"You're going to write him back?" Mads said.

"Under a fake name," Lina said.

"Diabolical," Holly said. "This should be good."

"That sounds like something I would do." Mads sighed. "Do you think Sean will come if I ask him?" Her mind was still on her party. *If only Sean would come,* she thought, *everything would be perfect.* For one thing, where Sean went, all the cool kids in school followed. For another thing, if he came to her party, it would mean he considered her worthy enough to show up at her house. And that was a step closer toward actually liking her.

Holly shrugged. "There's only one way to find out."

Mads got to her feet. "I'd better get up to the art room. I'm working on a portrait of Captain Meow-Meow. I'm having trouble capturing his sense of humor on paper." Captain Meow-Meow was her Siamese cat.

"Captain Meow-Meow has a sense of humor?" Lina said.

"Of course," Mads said. "If he could talk, he'd be Conan O'Brien."

"Funny, I never noticed that side of him," Holly said.

"See you at my house tonight," Lina said.

"See you." Mads walked into the school building and up to the third floor. The art room was empty. Late afternoon sun poured in through the skylights. She sat at a table and took out a photo of Captain Meow-Meow she'd taken with her new digital camera. She'd caught him in her favorite cat pose—stretched flat out on her bed, legs weirdly straight behind him. She picked up some pastels and started working.

She was concentrating so hard she forgot where she was. When someone came up behind her and said, "What's that, a monkey?" Mads jumped.

She turned around. A tall boy with straight brown hair and bangs looked down at her. "Sorry," he said. "I didn't mean to startle you." He wore a black t-shirt that he'd torn and put back together with safety pins. On the front, in DayGlo chartreuse, he'd painted a star with an X through it.

"It's not a monkey, it's a Siamese cat," Mads said. "See?" She showed him the photo she was trying to copy.

"What's her name?" the boy asked.

"His," Mads said. "He's a male. Captain Meow-Meow."

The boy laughed. "And what's your name—Sergeant La-La?"

"That would be cool," Mads said. "But no, it's Madison."

"Madison Markowitz?" the boy said. "Of The Dating Game? I'm Stephen Costello. A big fan. Huge fan."

"Thanks." Mads felt her face heating up with happy embarrassment. She nodded at his t-shirt. "Do you have something against stars?"

He plucked the shirt away from his body to see the Xed-out star better. "No. I just thought it looked cool. Well, I'll let you work. Are you making an entry for the Art Fair?"

Mads nodded. "Portraits. In pastels. What about you?"

He crossed the room to a drafting table and returned with a handful of sketches. He laid them out in front of Mads. They looked like plans for a stage set. "I'm doing an installation piece. It's going to be a guy's bedroom. I'm going to put in replicas of everything a teenage guy might have—posters, books, videos, games, CDs, magazines, clothes, a computer . . . all that junk."

"That's cool," Mads said. "Looks like a lot of work."

"It is, but it will be worth it. I'm hoping to make a statement about teen culture and pop culture in general."

"What's the statement?" she asked.

"Well, it might change as I work on the project. But right now it's about clutter. How pop culture clutters our minds so that we can't think clearly or even recognize what's important to us."

Wow, Mads thought. *He's deep.* So deep Mads was a little afraid to talk to him.

She studied the sketches more closely. They showed three walls made of cardboard, seven feet high, painted white, with a window cut out of one wall. The room would be filled with cardboard furniture he planned to build himself. "I'm going to paint a rug on the floor and everything," he said.

"It's like a giant dollhouse," Mads said.

"I'm going to put a video monitor here," he said, pointing to a sketched-in TV on a shelf. "And have it running the whole time, with images from commercials and videos and stuff on a loop."

"You'll win a prize for sure," Mads said. "Nobody else is doing anything like this." She looked him over, trying to guess where all this artistic ambition came from. He was thin and plain-faced, but there was so much confidence in his bearing and such a brainy look in his eyes that he seemed striking and almost handsome.

"What year are you?" she asked.

"Junior," he said. "My family moved here from London last year."

"But you don't have a British accent," Mads said.

"I'm not British," Stephen said. "We only lived there for three years. Before that we lived in New York."

"You must have had so many interesting experiences," Mads said.

"I guess," he said. "But it doesn't really matter where you live—Werner says the true adventure of life is in your mind and in your dreams."

"Who's Werner?" Mads asked, and immediately regretted it. What if Werner was super-famous, somebody everybody should know, like Shakespeare? What if she'd just said something stupid?

"He's a German philosopher. He wrote this book called *The Empty World*. I'll lend it to you if you want."

"Thanks." He didn't say it as if he thought she were an idiot, which she appreciated.

"Anyway, I knew lots of people in London who were always bored, even though there was tons of cool stuff to do all the time."

"I've lived in Carlton Bay since I was three," Mads said. "People think nothing ever happens here, but those people aren't paying attention. Like a few weeks ago I was at this party at a very elegant house—" She was thinking of Sean's Victorian house, which *was* elegant in its over-decorated way. "We were all drinking screwdrivers, of course, though *some* kids insisted on beer, and this senior, Alex, asked me to tell him the story of my life. Well, I closed my eyes and thought, What a question. What *is* the story of my life? What is life all about, anyway? Just thinking about it made me so dizzy I nearly got sick right there!"

This story had elements of truth in it, but Mads had added a philosophical twist to it that had never been there before. Mads *was* at a party, and Alex *did* ask her to tell him the story of her life, and she did nearly get sick right there. But not because of existential nausea. More like too many screwdrivers. The actual vomiting took place a few minutes later, in Sean's mother's room. Mads decided to spare Stephen those unnecessary details.

"Wow," Stephen said. "You've already had your first existential crisis. Very precocious."

"Thank you." Mads beamed. "For my age, I'm kind of a woman of the world. I mean, I wasn't before, but this year, things just started happening to me. There's one guy who was insanely in love with me—he even wrote a poem about me. Did you see it? He posted it on the library bulletin board."

"I must have missed it," Stephen said.

The boy she was describing—known as Yucky Gilbert—was a twelve-year-old freshman who occasionally wore a cape. More details Stephen was better off not knowing. "He wanted too much from me. I'm not ready to give my whole self up, heart and soul. I hate breaking guys' hearts, but what else can I do?"

Stephen gathered up his sketches and shook his head. "You sound like trouble, Madison. I'd better stay away from you."

Mads laughed. "You can call me Mads. All my friends do."

"Mads. The perfect name for a madwoman like you.

And I mean that as a compliment."

"Thank you. My father does say my mind has a logic all its own."

"My mother calls me St. Stephen the Serious. Once you've gotten to know me a little better, I'd like you to tell me if you think that's true."

"Do you want it to be true?" Mads asked.

"No." He sat down at a nearby table and laid out his sketches, studying them. He picked up a pencil and started drawing. No one spoke for several minutes. Then he stopped, his hair in his eyes, and said, "Will you tell me? Do you promise to tell me the truth?"

"Yes, I will. I promise."

Mads was afraid that on first impression, Stephen's mother was right. But what was so terrible about being serious? She thought it was kind of appealing.

3 Larissa Comes to Life

Look," Lina said. "He changed his ad!"

Holly and Mads were in Lina's bedroom after dinner. Lina showed them a personal ad from an online dating site called The List. The screen name said "beauregard" but the picture showed the blue-eyed, sincere face of their IHD teacher, Dan Shulman. Ever since she had discovered his ad, Lina had obsessed over every detail. What was he looking for? What were his secrets? Whenever he changed an entry, she pondered the meaning of it.

Lina had had a crush on Dan since the beginning of the school year, and it got stronger every day. Mads and Holly knew about it, of course, but they didn't realize how intense it was. And Lina couldn't share that with them. It was private.

"I want to read the ad," Mads said.

MAN SEEKING WOMAN
beauregard
ID#: 5344474
Age: 25
Occupation: teacher
Last great book I read: *Dubliners*, by James Joyce. The last line of "The Dead" gets me every time.
Most embarrassing moment: In third grade, when my older sister revealed to our entire school that I still slept with my blankie.
Celebrity I resemble most: Some people say Tobey Maguire, but I don't really look like a celebrity.
If I could be anywhere at the moment: Sailing down the California coast.
Song or album that puts me in the mood: "Get the Party Started" by Pink; anything by Elliott Smith or the Velvet Underground.

Favorite on-screen sex scene: Cartoon skunk Pepe Le Pew and the girl skunk who loves him, surrounded by hearts.

Best or worst lie I've ever told: When my sister asked me if I liked her boyfriend and I said yes, trying to be nice. Now they're married and I've got a soulless corporate shill for a brother-in-law.

The five items I can't live without: Nutter Butter cookies, my dictionary, a pen knife, my bike, Chapstick . . . and I love walnuts but I'm allergic to them.

In my bedroom you'll find: my bed, books, papers I should have graded long ago, old photos, notebooks full of unfinished stories and random scribbling, dirty socks, a rack full of old ties, three hats on a shelf, a guitar.

Why you should get to know me: I always try to do the right thing. I mean I really think about it. I'm very patient, except with my sister, the one person who knows how to push my buttons (in case you couldn't tell). I know lots of two-letter Scrabble words. I would love to "take you out to the ball game." I make a mean blueberry pie.

What I'm looking for: A friend to call for spur-of-the-moment adventures. An appreciative consumer of my cooking. A low-maintenance, non-material girl with a sense of humor. A sexy bookworm.

That's me, Lina thought. *A sexy bookworm.* Well, maybe she wasn't so sexy, but she *was* a bookworm. Every time she read his profile she fell for him a little more. She was the girl he was looking for. He just didn't know it yet.

Mads and Holly cracked up. "A sexy bookworm!" Mads squealed.

"I like the part where he says he wants to take you out to the ball game," Holly said.

"He still sleeps with his blankie!" Mads said.

"No, he doesn't," Lina said. "That was in third grade."

"Still," Mads said. "He's even geekier than I thought."

Lina didn't bother pointing out what mattered to her—the change he'd made in his ad. He changed "Last great book I read" from *Great Expectations* by Charles Dickens to *Dubliners* by James Joyce. The girls had read Joyce's *Portrait of the Artist as a Young Man* in English that year. Lina loved the strange, poetic language of it.

"I can't believe he likes Pink," Mads said, laughing. "Can you picture him dancing around his room at night to 'Get the Party Started'?"

Holly and Mads started dancing and singing, *"I-I-I-I'm comin' up so you better get the party started."* They collapsed in giggles on Lina's bed. Lina couldn't help laughing, too. It meant a lot to her, but at the same time she knew it was silly.

"Has Ramona seen the ad yet?" Holly asked. "She'll totally lose her mind. There's enough info in there for a year's worth of cult meetings."

"I don't think she knows about it," Lina said. "And I'm not going to tell her."

"Good thinking," Mads said. "She might lure him away by dying her hair pink."

Ramona Fernandez was in love with Dan, too. She was an out-there Goth girl who had no shame, which drove Lina crazy. Lina loved the way Dan dressed, in early-sixties suits, skinny vintage ties, and the occasional hat. But Ramona and her friends took their admiration a step further—*in the wrong direction*, Lina thought. They all wore skinny ties like Dan's and called themselves the Dan Shulman Cult. It was so embarrassing. Lina kind of liked Ramona, the more she got to know her. Ramona understood a side of Lina that her other friends never quite saw. But then Ramona would do something cringe-worthy, like sucking up to Dan in class, and Lina would shudder. She hoped she never came off the way Ramona did.

"So when are you going to write him back?" Mads asked. "Can I help you? 'Beauregard, my darling. Like you, I, too, am an admirer of Pepe Le Pew. His funny French accent, the white stripe down his back, his enticing *odeur*, to me it all adds up to Romance with a capital R.'" She and Holly giggled again.

"Very funny," Lina said. "You're too late. I've already

written something. Not that I'd trust it to you."

Lina called up an e-mail from her "Mail waiting to be sent" file. She'd been working on the e-mail for days, trying to get the tone exactly right. "What do you think?"

Dear Beauregard,
I found your ad intriguing. I've never answered an ad or done anything like this before. I'm a 22-year-old graduate student studying film. I love to read and I'm a terrible cook but I do like blueberry pie, Nutter Butters, Scrabble, and James Joyce. If you have time to write back, I'd love to hear from you. I'm up for any spur-of-the-moment adventures you have in mind.
—Larissa

"It's not nearly as funny as mine would have been," Mads said. "Who's Larissa?"

"I made her up," Lina said. "I can't use my real name or he might suspect it's me." Lina had chosen the name Larissa because it started with an L, like Lina, and it had a romantic, exotic quality she thought might appeal to Dan.

"Why is Larissa a film student?" Holly asked.

Lina shrugged. "I tried to come up with something easy to fake. If I said 'organic chemistry' he'd figure out I was lying pretty fast. But I've been to the movies. What's the big deal? I think I can fake being a film student."

"Just think," Mads said. "If he writes back, we can find out all kinds of stuff about him! You can ask him if he has favorite students or if he actually hates us! We can find out what he does after school. Maybe he's got a secret identity as a punk rocker—or a cross-dresser!"

"Mads, he's not a cross-dresser," Lina said.

"Send the e-mail, Lina," Holly said. "See what happens."

"Now? Should I do it now?" Lina asked, suddenly nervous.

She hesitated. The last time they did something like this it ended in a kind of disaster. They'd filled out a love quiz with jokey, sexy answers, signed it "Boobmeister Holly," and e-mailed it to Rebecca Hulse. The quiz spread all over the school and everyone started teasing Holly and calling her "the Boobmeister." Of course, *that* led to them starting The Dating Game, which had led to lots of other things, good and bad. . . . So had sending the quiz been good or bad, in the end? Lina couldn't say. It was too confusing.

"What if the e-mail isn't perfect?" Lina said. "I could probably make it better. . . ."

"You'll never send it if it has to be perfect," Holly said. "It's fine. Send it!"

"A week from now we'll all be laughing about his

cross-dressing tendencies," Mads predicted. "He wears size thirteen pumps. You wait and see."

Lina ignored her. "Okay. Here goes." She pressed SEND and "Larissa" came to life.

4 Nuclear Autumn

To:	hollygolitely
From:	your daily horoscope

HERE IS TODAY'S HOROSCOPE: CAPRICORN: Today your parents will embarrass you. (This one is a no-brainer—it works for every sign, every day of the year.)

utumn is unmatchable!" Mads complained. Holly had Mads and Lina over after school on Friday to work on matchmaking. Subject #1: Autumn Nelson.

"No one is unmatchable," Holly declared. She was surprised to hear herself say this. She wasn't quite sure she believed it.

"Autumn is," Lina said. "For one thing, she writes

every detail of her life on Nuclear Autumn." Autumn
didn't hold anything back: She ranted, she raved, she
insulted people, she had hissy fits. "What boy wants every
detail of his love life made public?"

"And she's such a drama queen," Mads said. "She has
a fit if she loses an eyelash."

"She's pretty cute, though," Holly said.

"Her personality totally negates it," Lina said. "Boys
don't like her. She's too high-maintenance."

"Well, we don't have much choice," Holly said. "Read
this." She logged on to Nuclear Autumn.

"This?" Mads asked. She read out loud in a whiny
Autumn voice. "'The stepmonster-in-waiting did it again.
She always has to have her way. Just because it's *her* birthday and *her* parents are visiting, we have to eat her fat
mother's homemade lasagna? Hello? It has *eggplant* in it. I
hate eggplant! Could she be more selfish?'"

"No, not that," Holly said. "Further down."

Why is everybody so into the stupid Dating Game? Or should I
call it The Waiting Game? Those girls have no idea what
they're doing! I asked them to match me up three
weeks ago but have I heard word one from those
byatches? No! If they're all such love experts and such
great matchmakers, then what's the holdup? I'm the

easiest case they've got! I want someone who's super-cute, smart, popular, athletic, funny, nice—did I say cute? That's all I ask. If those losers can't find a date for someone like me, then I say the whole thing is a sham! Boycott The Dating Game!

"Ouch," Lina said.

"She's so mean," Mads said. "Her ass is grass—and I'm the lawnmower." Mads struck a karate pose to indicate she was ready to get rough.

"There's no time for that," Holly said. "We've got to find her a date before she ruins our reps for good."

They scanned the questionnaires of available boys. "Who will be our sacrificial lamb?" Lina asked.

"I hate to do it to any of them," Holly said.

Most of the applicants used screen names, but a few used their real names and even sent in photos of themselves. Holly zeroed in on a boy she recognized from last year's science lab but didn't know well—Vince Overbeck. He had a placid face, an unruffled air about him. He was a wrestler—quiet, highly disciplined. In short, nothing like Autumn.

"What about this guy?" Holly asked.

"Vince Overbeck? Who's he?" Mads asked.

"I had him in my Algebra class last year," Lina said. "Quiet guy. The type you don't notice. He never talked in class but he got an A. Real smart."

"That sounds bad, Holly," Mads said. "Autumn will eat him alive!"

"I'm not so sure," Holly said. "Maybe Vince is just the guy she needs—someone quiet and nice, whose life could use a little shaking up. He might like the drama."

Lina and Mads stared at her, unconvinced.

"Do you guys have a better suggestion?"

"No," Mads admitted. "But can you deal with the consequences? What happens when we find poor Vince's bones in Autumn's locker—picked clean?"

"That won't happen," Holly said, but she sounded surer than she felt.

Quiz: Are You a Drama Queen?

Do you friends call you Your Royal Hissy Fit behind your back? Take this quiz and find out if you're easy-going or a touch too touchy.

1. **You break a nail on your way to school. You:**

    a ▶ don't notice.

    b ▶ stop at a nail salon to fix it—homeroom can wait.

    c ▶ sob quietly.

    d ▶ scream bloody murder.

2. **Your best friend goes to a party without you. You:**

a ▶ hope she had a good time.

b ▶ resolve to do the same to her next time.

c ▶ sob quietly.

d ▶ threaten to slit your wrists with a nail file.

3.   Your little sister ate the last Oreo (and they're your favorite).
     You:

     a ▶ shrug and figure you'll have some another time.

     b ▶ tell on her to your mother.

     c ▶ sob quietly.

     d ▶ take her favorite doll hostage until someone meets your
         Oreo demands.

4.   You got an F on an exam because you were partying instead of
     studying. You:

     a ▶ vow to do better next time.

     b ▶ ask to take a makeup exam.

     c ▶ sob quietly.

     d ▶ threaten to sue the school for discrimination against the
         handicapped—people with overactive social lives.

5.   You go to a party and another girl is wearing the same dress as
     you. You:

     a ▶ laugh it off.

     b ▶ go home and change.

c ▶ sob quietly.

d ▶ push her into the pool.

6. Your boyfriend says he doesn't like the sweater you're wearing. You:

   a ▶ tell him you like it and that's all that matters.

   b ▶ take it off immediately.

   c ▶ sob quietly.

   d ▶ cut it into tiny pieces and mail it to him covered in fake blood.

If you circled mostly A's, you're a DRAMA PEASANT, also known as a Cool Customer. Nothing bothers you too much because you've got your priorities straight. Sure, your friends secretly call you an ice queen behind your back, but even that doesn't rile you.

If you circled mostly B's, you're a PROBLEM SOLVER. When something goes wrong, you try to fix it—whether it's worth the trouble or not.

If you circled mostly C's, you're a SILENT SOBBER. You may not be a Drama Queen, but you've got bigger problems. Consider antidepressants or therapy.

If you circled mostly D's, start the hissy fit now because you're a full-blown DRAMA QUEEN. Congratulations, Your Highness.

"Rob! It's nice to see you again." Holly's mother, Eugenia,

greeted Rob at the front door of the Andersons' house. Holly hovered behind her, hoping to snatch Rob away and escape. It was Friday night. The Andersons were having a cocktail party, and Holly's parents had told her to have Rob stop by when he picked up Holly for the movies that night. Rob, thank god, was not wearing a t-shirt of any kind but a freshly pressed white button-down and khakis. Holly's mother, a thin, striking brunette, wore a long silk caftan and Holly wore a white cotton party dress printed with small yellow pineapples.

"Hello, Mrs. Anderson." Rob shook her hand.

"I told you before—call me Jen," Eugenia said. Holly's parents insisted on being called by their first names, Jen and Curt (short for Curtis), even by their own daughters. "You look so nice! Come in. I'll get Holly."

"I'm right here," Holly said.

"Hey, Holly." He made a move toward her, as if he might kiss her, then stopped, probably because her mother was standing there.

"Oh, go ahead and kiss her, it's okay," Jen said.

Rob looked uncertainly at Holly, who said, "Maybe later, Jen. Come on, Rob. Say hi to Curt." She took Rob's hand and led him into the spacious great room, which was filled with laughing, chattering adults. Ice clinked in their glasses as they nibbled canapés. The great room, which took up most of the first floor, had wooden beams and an angled ceiling like a fancy ski lodge.

"Hey, Rob!" Curt said warmly. "How are you, buddy?" He pumped Rob's hand. He was tall and broad-shouldered with curly, thinning blond hair, a ruddy face, and a thickening waist. He wore a blue blazer over his jeans and a pale-green polo shirt.

"Holly, the Fowlers want to say hello to you," Jen said, leading Holly toward the kitchen. Rob started to follow, but Curt said, "Stay here and chat a minute, Rob. You don't want to meet the Fowlers. They're dullsville."

"Curt! Not so loud!" Jen whispered. "Rob, maybe you could see if anyone needs a fresh drink."

"All right, Mrs. Anderson," Rob said.

"Jen," she said. "You'll get used to it."

"Jen, we're going to the movies," Holly protested. If she let her mother get them all caught up in the party, they'd never get out of there. Jen parked Holly in front of Gordon and Peggy Fowler, a tall, round-faced couple. Their daughter, Britta, was a junior at Rosewood.

Peggy gave Holly a hello kiss. "Hi, sweetie. You look blonder. Are you highlighting?"

"Not yet," Holly said. "It's still natural."

"She's lucky," Jen said. "If you saw what I go through to keep the gray from showing—" Peggy nodded knowingly.

"Britta tells us you've got a pretty high profile at Rosewood these days," Gordon said. "Some kind of dating Web site?"

Jen said, "She showed it to me one night. It's really very clever."

"It was a school project," Holly said. She scanned the room to see how Rob was doing. Curt was showing him how to pour a proper glass of Scotch.

"Well, listen, Holly," Peggy said. "I have a favor to ask you. You know, Britta's a junior now, and she's—well, she studies so much—"

"She's never had a boyfriend," Gordon finished. "Just hasn't been interested. Maybe you could take her along to a party or something one night? You two used to have fun together when you were little."

Holly vaguely remembered a five-year-old Britta swatting her and refusing to share her toys. "Uh, sure, I'll do what I can," Holly said.

"Nothing too wild," Peggy said. "She's still got her college applications to think of. Just something to help her relax a little bit, enjoy high school, maybe meet some nice new friends."

What had Britta told them about her? They seemed to think she was some kind of social superstar. If only they knew the truth. She and Lina and Mads were more popular than they'd been before they started the Dating Game. But they still struggled to get the attention of the most popular older kids.

"That's Holly's boyfriend over there," Jen said. "He's cute, isn't he?"

The Fowlers nodded and murmured nice things about Rob's darlingness.

"Come on, Holly. I need some help in the kitchen." Holly followed Jen into the kitchen. Jen plopped a tray of mini-quiches in her arms and pushed her back out. "Go! Go! Everybody's hungry!"

"Mom, we're trying to make a seven-thirty movie," Holly said. Jen ignored her. Holly caught Rob's eye as she circulated with the tray. He was pouring white wine for three women and seemed to be in no hurry to leave.

Jen sent her on another round with the hors d'oeuvres before Holly finally caught up with Rob, who was having a grand old time with Curt. Curt was telling Rob about another cocktail party they'd had once, when Holly performed for the guests.

"She sang the Alphabet Song, took off her shirt, and did a somersault," Curt said. "She was the hit of the party!"

"I was only four," Holly said. "You're telling that story as if it happened yesterday."

Curt had had a little too much Scotch. He put his arm around Rob and the two of them laughed.

"Curt, stop being a butthead," Holly said.

"Uh-oh, there she goes," Curt said. "Holly doesn't like it when you tease her. Or when she doesn't get her way. Did you ever see that look she gets, Rob? We call it her Grinch face."

"You mean, like this?" Rob twisted his face into an impatient scowl.

"Exactly!" Curt said. "I see you've had a few run-ins with the Grinch already." They laughed again, which only annoyed Holly more.

"You'll be seeing worse than the Grinch if we don't get out of here soon," Holly said.

"Come on, honey, we're having a great time," Curt said. "Rob and I are getting to know each other."

Holly glared at Rob. She could see he was torn between pleasing her and pleasing her dad. "Rob," she said. "What do *you* want to do? Go to the movies or help Curt hone his comedy act?"

"Better do what Grinchy wants," Curt said. He and Rob cracked up again.

"Fine," Holly said. "Yuk it up. You guys make a great team." She stormed off to her room.

"Holly!" Jen called after her. "Could you take the

caviar out of the fridge?"

She sat on her bed and counted the minutes until Rob came after her. Only five, but he could have come faster. Though she knew it was hard to get away from her father when he was in party mode.

"Holly, I'm sorry," Rob said. "You want to get out of here and go to the movie? Let's go."

"It's too late now," Holly said.

"Do you want to do something else then?"

"Let's just hide up here for a while."

"Okay." They lay down on her bed. He put his arms around her and held her. She nuzzled against him. She felt her anger melting away. It wasn't really his fault. She couldn't expect him to stand up to her parents. Still, she wished someone would, besides her.

There was a knock at the door. "Honey, are you coming back to the party?" It was Jen. "Everyone's asking for you."

"Maybe we'd better go back," Rob said.

"Is that what you want to do?" she asked.

"Well, I don't want to disappoint your parents." He hesitated. "But what do *you* want to do?"

She closed her eyes. "Nothing," she said. "Go back to the party and pour drinks. I'll be down in a minute."

●   ●   ●

"Hmm . . . I see trouble clouding those baby blues." Sebastiano Altman-Peck stared into Holly's eyes on Monday morning. Holly's locker was next to his, so she saw him at least twice a day. He was part of her routine, like brushing her teeth.

"The Great Sebastiano sees all. The patient is experiencing acute love-itis along with symptoms of severe Sebastiano withdrawal."

"Excuse me, Great Sebastiano, while I turn away from your penetrating gaze." Holly dialed the combination on her lock. "It's too early in the morning for this. What's Sebastiano withdrawal, anyway?"

"You haven't seen me for two whole days. It makes you cranky. Don't worry, it's perfectly normal. People crave me like cigarettes." Sebastiano rummaged through his locker until he found a long red scarf. "There you are," he said to the scarf as he wrapped it around his neck. Fully dressed at last, he slammed his locker shut and leaned against it. "Now. What's with this love trouble? I want the dirt. I can wait all day."

"No, you can't," Holly said. "The bell's going to ring in about two seconds."

"If I want to stand here and wait for you to spill your guts, I'll do it." He closed his eyes and rubbed his temples like a mind-reader. "The Great Sebastiano sees a hunky brown-haired boy . . . a red baseball cap . . . a pair of plastic swim goggles . . . Could it be—? Yes, it's star swimmer and Holly-adorer Rob Safran." He opened his eyes to confront Holly. "You might as well confess. I'll get it out of you sooner or later."

"Okay," Holly said. "Something is bothering me just a microbit. One teeny, tiny little thing that's not the least bit important at all."

"Ah-ha," Sebastiano said. "The Great Sebastiano is always right. And that tiny little thing would be—? It's the red baseball cap, isn't it. It makes him look like Ronald McDonald. Too bad, because he's a hottie when his hair isn't flattened into a heinous fringe around his head."

"I can live with the cap," Holly said. "But there's something else. Before he kisses me he says, 'Mind if I kiss you?' every single time."

"Really? That's uptight of him. Have you tried ordering him to stop? Or are *you* too uptight?"

"I'm not uptight!" Holly said.

"You're just chicken," Sebastiano said.

"And he's spineless," Holly said. "He always wants to do whatever I want, or my parents want, but he never says what *he* wants."

"Hmm . . . Here's my diagnosis. What you've got is a Boy Who Likes You Too Much," Sebastiano said. "He likes you so much he's afraid he'll do something wrong. His love for you has turned him into a wimp."

"Is there a cure?" Holly said. "I really like him. And he's only being nice."

"Right. Nice. Nothing sexier than nice," Sebastiano said. "What about Mo Basri? I saw him checking you out the other day. Don't underestimate your appeal, Holly. You're smart, you're sweet, but you have a dab of eau-de-bad-girl behind your ear, if you know what I mean. Rreow!"

Holly paused. "Mo Basri was really checking me out?" Mo was a senior with glossy black hair and a sharp nose. He was popular and a little slick.

"Watched you walk from here to the gym for three straight minutes without taking his eyes off you," Sebastiano said.

Holly let this sink in. After a long, blah winter, spring was here. Rebirth. New possibilities. Love in the air and all that. Maybe it was time for a change . . . in boyfriends.

5 Beauregard Writes Back

Lina, scoot down," Sebastiano yelled over the commotion in the Swim Center. Lina slid down the bench to make room for Sebastiano, who wanted to sit next to Holly. Rosewood's varsity swim team had a big meet against Draper that day, and Lina had joined Holly and Mads to watch. Rob and Sean were key members of the team.

"Oh my god, I've never seen Sean in a bathing suit before," Mads said. She dropped her head to her knees.

"I'm hyperventilating. He's so cute."

"Deep breaths, Mads, deep breaths," Lina said, rubbing Mads' back. Shouts and the shriek of a whistle echoed off the tile walls and the smell of chlorine sharpened the air.

"Go Rob!" Holly shouted as Rob got ready to start the freestyle relay.

"Hooray for Holly's honey!" Sebastiano shouted.

"Mads, the race is about to start," Lina said. Mads sat up, looking a little woozy.

"Is this spot taken?" Walker Moore hovered beside Lina, notepad and pen in hand. Lina shook her head and patted the seat.

"Thanks." Walker sat down and crossed his long legs. He had cut his dreadlocks, which he used to wear tied back, into short spikes all over his head. He and Lina had gone out once, on an ill-fated double date with Holly and a jerk named Jake. Lina liked Walker, but not that way. Not the way she liked Dan Shulman.

A whistle blew and the relay race started. Walker focused his attention on the pool. "Covering the meet for the paper?" Lina shouted over the din.

"Yeah," he replied. "We've got a good team this season. Maybe a shot at the championship."

"Go Sean, go Sean!" Mads screamed. Lina suppressed

the urge to roll her eyes. Sean wasn't even swimming yet. He was perched at the edge of the pool, waiting for Rob to finish his leg of the race and touch the wall.

Rob and the swimmer from Draper were neck and neck. Rob touched the wall, and Sean dove in and took the lead.

"Aaaaahh!" Mads squealed. "He's swimming! Go! Go!"

Walker jotted something in his notebook and glanced at Lina. "Is she always like this?" he asked.

"Pretty much," Lina said.

Sean brought Rosewood into the lead. All the rest of the team had to do was keep pace. They did, and Rosewood won the relay. The home crowd went crazy.

The swim center quieted down as the teams prepared for the next race. Someone tapped Lina on the shoulder. Lina turned around to see a green-eyed senior with short, wavy red hair—Kate Bryson, the editor-in-chief of the *Seer*.

"Hi, Lina," Kate said. They'd never actually spoken before, so Lina wondered how Kate knew her name. "Hey, Walker. Lina, I've wanted to talk to you for a while. We really need a girl covering sports and I think you'd be great."

"Me? Why?"

"I know you can write—I've seen some of your stuff on that Web site you and your friends have," Kate said. "And haven't you published in *Inchworm*, too?" Lina nodded. *Inchworm* was one of the school literary magazines. Dan was the faculty advisor and Ramona Fernandez the executive editor. They'd recently published a poem of Lina's.

"And you're a kick-ass field hockey player, so you get the sports thing," Kate added. Lina played field hockey in the fall. "Plus Walker recommended you."

Lina turned to Walker in surprise. He grinned and shrugged. Lina was flattered. Somebody actually thought of her as a writer. Or at least a potential writer.

"So will you do it?" Kate asked.

"Sure, I'll give it a try," Lina agreed.

"Good. We've got a staff meeting tomorrow at three-thirty. Show up and I'll give you your first assignment."

"Thanks, Kate." She turned to thank Walker, but another race had started and he was closely watching the pool.

"What was that all about?" Mads asked.

"I'm going to be a sports reporter," Lina said.

"Cool!" Mads passed the word on to Holly and Sebastiano, who'd been watching the scene curiously. Sebastiano gave her a thumbs-up. "That's my dream job," he shouted past Holly and Mads. "Well, after photographer, shoe designer, famous non-starving artist, and flamboyant rock star. And ambassador to France. But I'm sure you'll love it."

Lina turned back to watch the race, but it was over. *Uh-oh*, she thought. *I'd better learn to pay attention at these things.*

The first thing Lina did when she got home, as always, was check her e-mail. It had been a week since she'd written to "Beauregard" as "Larissa," and she hadn't heard anything back. But today was the magic day.

To: Larissa
From: Beauregard
Re: The List
Dear Larissa,
Thanks for answering my ad. I'm sorry it took me so long to get back to you but to my surprise, my ad has received a lot of responses. It took a while just to wade through them all. But I liked yours the best. It was short and simple but nice.
So here's a little bit more about me. I'm a high school teacher. I love the kids but I'm not crazy about the subject I got stuck with. It's called Interpersonal Human Development, and even though the school year is two-thirds over I'm still not sure what that's supposed to mean. I'd much rather teach literature, but those jobs are hard to find right now, especially around here. I'm originally from Iowa City, but I came west to go to

college and I fell in love with the Bay Area, just like
   everybody else.
What about you? I think it's so cool that you're studying film.
   Where are you studying? I'm a huge Jarmusch fan, and
   the Coen brothers, of course, but I like Tarantino, too,
   with reservations. Who's your favorite filmmaker? I
   could talk about movies all day. I hope you'll write back
   soon.
—Beauregard

Lina could hardly believe what she had contained
inside her computer. She'd already learned so much she
never knew about him! She'd suspected that he didn't like
teaching IHD, so it was satisfying to find out she was
right. And he was from Iowa! That was so cute. Lina had
never been there, but she pictured golden wheat and
green cornfields. What kind of place was Iowa City? Did
people ride tractors down the street?

She read the e-mail a second time, and a third. She
didn't know who Jarmusch was, but at least she'd heard of
Quentin Tarantino and the Coen Brothers. She IM'ed
Holly and Mads.

linaonme: guess what? beauregard wrote back!
mad4u: no way! What did he say?

> linaonme: he said he was swamped with e-mails but he liked
> mine the best.
> hollygolitely: I've got to see this. can we come over?
> linaonme: come over after dinner. I'll write him back now, and
> maybe he'll answer by then.

Lina wanted to be alone for now so she could compose her first answer carefully. She didn't want to get caught in any traps she couldn't write her way out of. *You are Larissa,* she told herself. She grabbed a silk scarf from her dresser to put herself in a glamorous mood. *You are twenty-two. You're super-smart but not show-offy about it. You're beautiful but nice. You are perfect. You're Dan's dream girl.*

> Dear Beau,
> May I call you that, for short? Beauregard sounds so stuffy.

No, delete that last sentence, she decided. She didn't want to insult him in the first paragraph. She changed it to:

> Beauregard takes so long to type. I was pleased to receive
> your e-mail.

Now what? Answer his questions. But how? She needed to do a little research. She went online and

Googled "Jarmusch" to find out who that was. Jim Jarmusch, a seminal independent filmmaker who started out in the 1980s. First major film, *Stranger Than Paradise*. Often works in black-and-white. That was enough info to start with. Now, where was she studying?

She found a film department at Berkeley, so that was a possibility . . . Santa Cruz was too far away . . . Aha. San Francisco State had a grad program. Perfect. She knew the city fairly well, since Carlton Bay was only an hour north of it. And her father, a banker, went to work there every day. Now back to her e-mail.

Dear Beau,

May I call you that, for short? Beauregard takes so long to type. I was pleased to receive your e-mail. I have a few free moments to write you back before I'm off to a café to read up on film theory. I'm studying for my masters degree at San Francisco State. The film department here is so intellectual. We watch black-and-white movies all the time. I guess you must have seen *Stranger Than Paradise*, if you like Jarmusch. I love black-and-white movies, too. Of course, Quentin Tarantino usually works in color but I like his movies as well. Actually, I guess most movies are in color these days. It's hard to find a good one in black and white.

So anyway, I grew up in the Bay Area, and that's about it.
    Please write back soon—I'd love to read more about
    your life. What is the school where you work like? Do
    you have any favorite students?
—Larissa

Hello Larissa,
Feel free to call me Beau. Can I call you Lara for short? Like
    the heroine of *Doctor Zhivago*. Now there's a good
    movie, and in color, too.
(Your e-mail was so funny! "I guess most movies are in
    color." I'm glad you have a sense of humor. All my
    favorite people do.)
Let's see, you asked about the school where I teach. Well, it's
    an interesting place. It's a public high school, pretty
    progressive. Or, as the principal says, it's an "assessment-
    driven, cross-curricular, inquiry-centered school
    designed to maximize the students' competencies as
    impactfully as possible." My friend Camille and I call
    him Rod, because he's got such a stick up his butt. Not
    to his face, of course. We want to keep our jobs, at least
    for now.
Anyway, it's supposed to be a magnet school for the smart
    kids in the area, but this is a fairly ritzy town, and all the
    parents think their kids are geniuses. So they prep them

for the test to get into the magnet school and a lot of them get in. But most of them are far from geniuses, trust me. I do like some students better than others, but I try not to let it show.

The teachers are a mixed lot. There's this one poor old geometry teacher named Mildred. She's got a glass eye, she's overweight, and she's getting up there in years— she's got to be close to sixty. The kids call her "Mildew" and "Sleep-Eez" behind her back, but she's actually a nice lady. The art teacher is this odd, super-skinny guy with a long mustache. He's hung over almost every morning and he smokes like a chimney, but he's good for a laugh. He's been at the school for twenty years. At times the bitterness shows. God, I think I'd shoot myself if had to teach there that long.

Well, I've really rambled on. Hope I didn't bore you. Teaching at a suburban high school isn't nearly as glamorous as being a big-city film student. Write back soon, if you have time, and tell me more about yourself. You saw the "Five things I can't live without" in my ad. What are yours?

—Beau

"Wow, Frank Welling is hung over every day?" Mads said. He was the art teacher Dan had described. "No wonder he's so cranky in the mornings."

"This is amazing," Holly said. She and Mads huddled around Lina's computer that evening, reading the secret thoughts of their teacher. "It's a gold mine of inside information!"

"I can't believe he calls Mr. Alvarado 'Rod,'" Mads said. The principal's real name was John Alvarado, and he did spout a lot of educational jargon. "That is so funny. Rod. Rod Alvarado. He *is* very stiff." She drew herself up straight and imitated his voice. "'It's critical that the facilitators of this proactive mission triangulate their methodologies.'"

Holly and Lina laughed. "Who's this 'Camille' he mentions?" Holly asked.

"It must be Mademoiselle Barker," Lina said. The pretty young French teacher. Lina hadn't realized that she and Dan were such good friends. She'd often wondered if there wasn't something—a flirtation at least—between them.

"What's the deal with her, anyway?" Mads said.

"They can't be dating, or he wouldn't be writing to Larissa," Holly said.

Lina took comfort in that. But she still had her suspicions.

"I've got to write him back again," Lina said. "What should I say?"

"Ask him if any of his students have crushes on him," Mads said.

"No!" Lina said.

"That way you'll know if he's on to you," Mads said.

"No," Lina repeated.

"Ask him what he thinks of Goth girls," Holly said, thinking of Lina's friend and rival, Ramona.

"Too obvious," Lina said. "I don't want him to realize that I know him."

"All right then, keep it simple," Holly said. "Tell him your favorite foods and colors and all that, and ask his. And see where that takes you."

"Good idea." Lina started composing her reply.

Dear Beau,
You're right—film school is a lot more glamorous than high
    school. How could it not be? I'd die if I had to go
    through high school again.

"That's good," Holly said. "Piper says that all the time." Piper was Holly's older sister, who was away at college.

"What about the five things you can't live without?" Mads said. "Let's see, there's gummi worms, peanut butter, your day-of-the-week underwear—"

"Mads! I'm not going to tell him about that." She did

love gummi worms and peanut butter and her day-of-the week underwear, with a different pastel color for each day. She also loved Frosted Teddy Grahams and her old Raggedy Ann doll, but she wasn't about to tell *him* that. Larissa wouldn't like those things. Larissa was too sophisticated.

> The five things I can't live without are my Chanel no. 5 perfume, my red nail polish, my *Encyclopedia of Film*, my dark glasses, and a pair of high heels.

"Wow, that's glam," Mads said.

"You should add peanut butter," Holly said. "He said he loves Nutter Butters. It gives you something in common."

"Okay." Lina changed the high heels to peanut butter. It added a nice touch of humility.

> I can tell from the way you talk about your school that you are a good teacher. I'll bet the students really appreciate you. You're a good writer, too. Have you ever thought of writing a novel? I think I'd like to try it myself someday. What are you doing now? Are you at home, grading papers? Are you out somewhere, seeing friends? I'm just curious. I'm writing to you on my laptop at a café, watching all the people come and go. I can see the lights of the Bay Bridge

twinkling in the distance. This really is a beautiful city. Good night, Beau. Write back soon.

—Lara

"Wow, Lina, that's beautiful," Mads said. "It's almost like a poem."

Lina hoped Dan would be just as impressed.

Mads and Holly had gone home by the time Dan responded. Lina was glad. His answer was short and sweet, and she wanted to keep it private.

Dear Lara,

It's late at night, and I know I might regret this in the morning . . . but I have to tell you, you are amazing. You have such a beautiful way of looking at life. I don't want to rush things, but I sincerely hope we will meet someday.

Yours, Beau

6 Portrait of the Artist as a Teenage Girl

To: mad4u
From: your daily horoscope

HERE IS TODAY'S HOROSCOPE: VIRGO: People often underestimate you, but you're determined to show them they're wrong. It's a lost cause, but I guess I can't stop you from trying.

Stand against that white wall," Mads told Holly. She pressed Holly against the wall in the art room. "Okay, look right at me," Mads instructed. "Don't smile. Good." She took a picture with her new digital camera. "Now let's try a few where you're smiling."

Stephen worked on the other side of the room, constructing his bedroom installation. Mads could feel him half-watching and half-listening.

"Why don't you pose her like Venus?" he suggested. "Like that famous painting."

Mads knew the one he meant, where Venus is standing on a giant seashell. "You mean, naked?" Mads asked.

"I'm not posing naked, even for you, Mads," Holly said.

"No, but looking as if she's coming out of the sea, maybe a fan blowing her hair back—" Stephen said.

"Sorry, but that's not my vision of Holly," Mads said. "And, anyway, I'm not sure I could draw that."

Stephen shrugged. "She reminds me of that painting, that's all."

Mads stopped and looked at him, surprised. Did Stephen have a thing for Holly? He had turned back to his work, so Mads couldn't tell. But saying a girl looks like Botticelli's *Venus* was a pretty high compliment, especially coming from an arty guy like him.

She looked through the photos she'd taken and chose a pretty shot of Holly with a half-smile on her face, tugging on a strand of hair. She loaded it onto the computer and printed out a copy to work from.

"Can I stay and watch you work for a few minutes?" Holly asked.

"Sure," Mads said. "You can help me plan my party.

Should I send out real invitations or e-vites? If I go with snail mail I've got to send them by tomorrow or people won't get them in time." Stephen was hammering now, so he couldn't hear them talking. She didn't want him to think she was frivolous, an empty head full of nothing but party details.

"E-vites are fine," Holly said. "Are your parents going to be there?"

"Duh. Do you think they'd let me have a party without total supervision? Not only will my parents be there, but my Aunt Georgia and Uncle Skip are coming to keep them company. I talked them out of inviting the teachers at least. But I've got to find a way to keep the adults from poisoning the party with their toxic bring-down rays."

Mads took out her pastels and clipped a thick piece of paper to an easel. "This is a great picture of you, Holly," she said.

Holly leaned over to look at it. "You think? My nose looks so big."

"No, it doesn't," Mads said. "You have an elegant nose."

"It's a good thing you took my picture today and not tomorrow," Holly said. "I feel a giant zit coming on. It's sitting just below the surface of my skin, waiting for the perfect moment to pop out and ruin my life."

"You never get zits."

"Oh yeah? What do you call this?" Holly pointed to a tiny red dot near her hairline.

Mads squinted to see it. "I call that invisible. You want to see a zit? Take a look at—"

The hammering stopped. Mads clammed up. She felt funny talking about zits and noses in front of Stephen. She was afraid it would make her seem silly. She sighed loudly and slapped Holly's photo against her thigh.

"Isn't this ridiculous? Here you are sitting right in front of me, and I'm drawing you from a photo. It's a perfect example of how technology distances us from real life."

"What?" Holly said. "Can we get back to zits please, because I don't know what you're talking about."

"But I need the photo so I can work on the drawing when you're not around," Mads continued. "Oh, the terrible demands of modern life."

"You'd be lost without your cell phone, your iPod, and your laptop, and you know it," Holly said.

"Mads, that reminds me," Stephen called from across the room. Aha—he *was* listening. He rummaged through his backpack and pulled out a book. "I brought this for you, in case you're interested." He crossed the room and laid the book on her table. *The Empty World* by Berndt Werner.

Mads lightly touched the cover. "Thanks, Stephen. This is that philosopher you said you liked, right?"

Holly reached for the book. "Hey, my sister Piper is reading that for her philosophy seminar." She read the back cover and added, "Wow, Mads, this is heavy stuff. You sure you can handle it?"

Mads shot her a dirty look. "Of course I can. I'm very interested in philosophy."

"You can give it back when you're done with it," Stephen said, heading back toward his work area. "But take your time." He started hammering again.

"What's going on?" Holly whispered to Mads. "The only philosophy you're interested in is The Collected Wisdom of Sean Benedetto. Or so I thought."

"That's not true," Mads whispered back. "I'm interested in lots of things."

"Like Stephen," Holly said. "I know what you're doing up here after school every day. You're flirting with him!"

"No, I'm not!" Mads flushed red. She wasn't flirting with Stephen. She just liked talking to him. And she didn't think he'd waste his time talking to an airhead, so she tried to show him her more serious side. It was a good thing. Her serious side could use a little development.

"You're wrong, Holly," she said. "I'm still into Sean.

I'm just trying to improve myself, that's all."

"Okay, okay, I believe you," Holly said. "Don't get upset. Your face is redder than this crayon." She picked up a red pastel crayon. It left a rosy dust on her fingers.

Do I have a crush on Stephen? Mads wondered. She pushed the question out of her mind. Better not to think about it, she decided—and then she went right on thinking about it.

Why would a boy like Stephen be interested in me? He's so serious and I'm so flighty. . . . The harder I try to be serious, the flightier I am! Well, I'm *not* going to talk about this with anyone, not even Holly or Lina. They already think I'm crazy to be in love with Sean. Here I am, crushing on another guy who will never like me back. . . . I'll look like a mental case, or at least pathetic. They'll just make a big deal out of nothing. And that's what it is— nothing.

7 A Match Made in Purgatory

To:	Hollygolitely
From:	your daily horoscope

HERE IS TODAY'S HOROSCOPE: CAPRICORN: You know that old saying, "No good deed goes unpunished"? Prepare to take a licking.

Nuclear Autumn: Keeping You Informed of the Latest Developments in the Life of Autumn Nelson

Holly, Lina, and Madison finally got off their butts and set up a
date for me. They told me to meet this guy—let's call
him Mr. V—at Vineland. I didn't know the guy, or
anything about him. I was having doubts—serious
doubts. I called everybody I knew to see if they knew
who he was. I didn't want to be seen in public with

some loser! But Holly convinced me to take a chance. She said love was all about laying it on the line and taking risks, blah blah blah. So I go to Vineland and I see this guy sitting there. Okay, I have to admit his first impression didn't blow me away. He was just a guy. Or so I thought.

I sat down and we started talking and I told him all about myself. I told him how Chloe, aka the stepmonster-in-waiting, aka Dad's girlfriend, was ruining my life by spending all Dad's money on herself, and how Mom's being such a bitch lately and everybody in the family hates me but they all just lo-o-ove my little half-sister, Lily, isn't she cute? Well, who isn't cute at age six, I ask you? You should have seen me at six, I was irresistible. Time waits for no one, little Lily. You'll find out someday. She'll grow up to be a total delinquent—will they still get all googly-eyed over her then? And then there's Rebecca, my former best friend who spends all her time with her new boyfriend David and totally neglects me in my time of need!

Anyway, Mr. V sat and listened to me for two and half hours before he finally said he was hungry and took me to the cutest little Mexican place right near the beach. We had enchiladas and talked some more about how I should redecorate my room and whether or not I could get into a decent college if I flunk Geometry this year. He paid for dinner and he was so sweet and by the end of the evening I looked at him and thought, You know what? This guy is gorgeous! I mean, it just hit me like that, he's the kind of cute you don't notice right away but it sneaks up on you and wham!—you're in love!

We walked on the beach, even though it was chilly, and then he drove me home. We kissed in the car and he is the best kisser ever. I don't want to hear about any other boy and the way he kisses. Mr. V cannot be topped. Period. Then he walked me to my door. I was so happy I couldn't sleep. Chloe saw me when I walked in all glowy and said, "What's with you? Your cheeks are all flushed," and I said, "It's called love, you gold-digging slime, and you wouldn't know it if it slapped you in the face."

So, my devoted followers, it was the best date ever and I think I'm in love. Thanks to Holly and the other two for hooking us up. Your names will be entered in the Nuclear Autumn Hall of Fame, along with the colorist who totally saved me when my hair came out orange that time, the girl who found my gym bag when I left it in the locker room and returned it to me without taking my new yoga pants, and the doctor who did my nose job. You get the Autumn Seal of Approval! XXOO

"Wow, Holly," Mads said. "This is our biggest success ever! You made Autumn happy, and everybody in school knows it!"

"At first I thought it was all in her mind," Holly said. "I mean, how could Vince have enjoyed that date? All she did was talk about herself. But look—he really seems to like her."

Holly, Lina, and Mads gazed across the courtyard to the bench where Vince—the mysterious Mr. V—sat listening to Autumn. He looked like a different person. He glowed.

"It's funny," Holly said. "He really does seem handsomer all of a sudden." Of course, a lot of guys seemed handsomer to her lately.

"I guess he just wanted someone to pay attention to him," Lina said.

"Hi, girls." Mo Basri stopped by their bench. Holly straightened up. Was Mo really interested in her, as Sebastiano had said? She thought she'd caught him watching her a couple of times, but this was the first time he'd ever come up to talk to her.

"I read all about you on Nuclear Autumn," Mo said. "How do you girls know so much about love?"

He said "girls," but he was looking at Holly the whole time.

"Do you think you could give me some advice?" Mo asked. "A friend of mine has a problem."

Holly struggled not to glance at Lina and Mads. She could feel them next to her, suppressing giggles. "Well, we don't know everything, but we can try to help. What's up?"

"My friend likes this girl, but she has a boyfriend," Mo said. "Should he let her know how he feels, or leave her alone? Is it uncool to tell a girl you like her if she's taken?"

Interesting. And very transparent. Did this mean Mo's "friend"—obviously Mo himself—had a crush on Holly? Holly knew that if she looked at Mads and Lina now they'd start cracking up. And that would ruin everything. So she must not look at them. Danger. Danger. Do not turn head to left!

"Well, I guess it depends, Mo," Holly said. "Sometimes a girl has a boyfriend but she feels ready to move on. Is she sending you any signals?"

"This girl's kind of mysterious," Mo said. "I'm not sure how to read her."

"Hmm. I guess you might as well take a shot. You've got nothing to lose. If she's still into her boyfriend, the worst she can do is say no. If she's not and says yes, then it was worth the risk, right?"

Mo grinned. "Right. Thanks, Holly. Oh, one more

thing. I don't have this girl's phone number. Is it okay to ask a girl out by e-mail?"

"If you don't have her number, sure, I guess it's okay," Holly said.

"Cool," Mo said. "See you later." He crossed the courtyard and went into the school. Lina and Mads started laughing as soon as he was out of earshot.

"Guess you'll be getting an e-mail from him soon," Lina said.

"You think so?" Holly said.

"How obvious could he be?" Mads said.

"We'll see," Holly said, but she had a feeling they were right.

"You're good at giving advice, Holly," Mads said. "You really sounded like you knew what you were talking about! You should do an advice column on the site."

"You could be the Love Ninja," Lina said. "Attacks love problems by stealth!"

An advice column. Holly liked the idea. It would be fun to obsess over other people's problems for a change.

"I'll do it," Holly said. "The Love Ninja . . . It's a nice combination of sentiment and violence. Like love itself."

A few days later, after she finished her homework, Holly logged onto the Dating Game blog to check her inbox. It was jammed with matchmaking requests and letters to the Love Ninja. They'd announced the column on The Dating Game site with a link to Nuclear Autumn. Holly sifted through the e-mails, chose the best ones, and wrote her first column.

Dear Love Ninja,

My best friend is very pretty. Boys are always hitting on her. One night at a club these two boys came up to us. The cuter one started flirting with my friend and his friend asked me to dance. When we got back, my friend was gone. Since that night, the cute boy has been dating my friend but I haven't heard a word from his buddy. What happened?

—Second Banana

Dear Second Banana,

What happened is you've been the victim of the old wing play. I think it comes from soccer terminology, or maybe ice hockey. The cute boy liked your friend and asked his pal to be the "wing man." In other words, he pretended to like you in order to distract you—so his friend could get some face-time with your girlfriend. It's one of those sneaky boy tricks that you have to watch out for. Some boys roam in packs like dogs and take turns playing

wing man for each other as the situation arises. It
stinks, doesn't it? Now that you know, warn others!
—Love Ninja

I really am good at this, Holly thought. *Look how much
effect I'm having on everybody's lives! I'm making people happy left
and right. Solving their problems. Helping them face reality and find
love. And the more I do it, the better I get at it. By the end of the school
year I could be as wise as Dr. Drew Pinsky.*

Her computer beeped to let her know another e-mail
had come in.

To: Love Ninja
From: Mbasri
Re: question for you
Hey Holly,
The Kevin Eleven are playing the Rutgers Roadhouse this
        weekend. Want to check it out one night? Maybe
        Saturday? They really rock.
Mo
P.S. The advice you gave my friend the other day was really
        smart.

Holly felt excited and nervous. She *knew* Mo was
interested in her, and she was right. But what should she

do? She was Rob's girlfriend. She couldn't just go out to concerts with other guys.

Or could she? After all, what was the big deal? She was only sixteen. She and Rob weren't *married*. And she really had no reason to think Mo was asking her as anything other than a friend. Deep down—not even so deep down—she knew better, of course. But she told herself that going to the show wouldn't mean anything.

She shouldn't have to think about this at all. She should be free! And that's when she realized that she wasn't facing the truth. Rob wasn't "it." He couldn't be. If he were, would she be having this conversation with herself? No, she'd reject Mo immediately. If Rob were "it," she'd know by now.

That left her with a big problem. She had to dump Rob. But how? She really liked him. She didn't want to hurt him. And she didn't want him to hate her. She wanted to stay friends with him *and* date other guys.

This was a job for the Love Ninja. Too bad she had no answer for her own problem.

I'll take it to the blog, she thought. A Dating Game poll. A few good solutions usually turned up among the garbage and jokes. But she had to disguise it so Rob wouldn't figure out what was going on. So she composed a fake letter to the Love Ninja.

Dear Love Ninja,

My girlfriend is very sweet but too clingy, and I've got a crush
    on another girl. I don't want to hurt her feelings, but I
    need my freedom. Is there any way to dump her without
    hurting her?

—Jailbird

Dear Jailbird,

Your problem is a common one, but hard to solve. I'm going
    to take it to the readers and see if they have any advice
    for you. Good luck!

—Love Ninja

Dear Readers: The Love Ninja needs your help! What's the
    best way to dump someone—without hurting his or her
    feelings?

jen88: There's no way to do it without hurting her. Just get it
    over with fast.

koala: Jailbird, is your real name Jonathan? Are you trying to
    dump me????

sami666: Lies, lies, and more lies. Tell her you're dying,
    you're moving to Siberia, you're becoming a monk.
    Anything to get her off your back. By the time she
    figures out that you lied, it will be too late.

poydog: write her a letter. If you dump her in person and she

starts crying, you might weaken and change your mind.
spoony: tell her you love her so much it hurts—literally. You're
on painkillers all the time, and the doctors say if you
don't stop seeing her you'll be a vegetable by the time
you're 18.
dollface: Before dropping bad news on anyone, it's a good
idea to feed them. Make a nice meal for her, then gently
tell her you need space. She'll be hurt, but her full
stomach will help blunt the pain.

All right, one sensible answer out of six, not bad.
Holly decided to take dollface's advice. She and Rob
would go on a picnic together—with all of Rob's favorite
foods. Holly felt a pang when she thought of the way he'd
forced down that Sham Ham sandwich, just for her.
Maybe she shouldn't be so quick to dump him. But no, it
was the only humane thing to do. It would hurt him much
more if she cheated on him.

This wasn't going to be easy.

"Where should we put the blanket?" Rob asked. He pointed
at a patch of grass and said, "How about over there?
Unless you want to put it somewhere else." It was late
afternoon, and she and Rob had driven to La Paz State
Park for the big breakup picnic.

"No, that spot is fine," Holly said.

"As long as it's okay with you," Rob said. "I mean, it's your picnic. Maybe you were thinking of a sunnier spot."

"This spot is plenty sunny." Holly tried to keep a lid on her annoyance. Did everything have to be a U.N. debate?

She unfolded the picnic blanket and opened the basket. "Ham sandwich?" she offered. "It's real this time. I promise."

"Thanks." Rob bit into the sandwich and nodded. "Mmm," he said through a mouthful, "blows that Sham stuff away."

"Glad you like it." She'd made the sandwiches herself, with lettuce, tomato, mustard, and fresh country bread from the best bakery in town. She'd also packed pasta salad, shrimp salad, fruit salad, iced tea, and homemade brownies for dessert.

"Wow, Holly, this is so nice of you," Rob said, settling back on the blanket. "What's the occasion?"

"No occasion," Holly said. "Do I need a reason to do something nice for my boyfriend?"

Rob appeared to think this over for a second, which annoyed her even more. "Well, you're usually pretty nice, but not this nice. Not that you're not very, very nice. But this is above and beyond."

He wore a t-shirt that said, BORN TO BE MILD, with a

cartoon of a lamb on it. The highly irritating sight of it gave Holly courage.

They finished their suppers. Rob polished off three brownies, lay on his back, closed his eyes, and rubbed his stomach contentedly. It was time.

"You know, Rob, I really like you," Holly said.

"I really like you, too," Rob said. He opened his eyes and turned toward her, reaching out to pat her hand but slapping her knee instead.

"Sometimes I forget how young we are," Holly said. "We're still really young."

"Yep. Whole lives ahead of us," Rob said. He closed his eyes again and let the sun warm his face.

"Too young to confine ourselves to one, uh, path," Holly went on. "One academic track, one career path, one, you know, person."

"Uh-huh." His eyes were still closed. It was hard to tell what he was thinking.

"Do you ever feel like you need, I don't know, more space?" Holly asked. "More time to yourself, to do what you want?"

"Sure."

"I feel that way, too, sometimes," Holly said. "That's why I think maybe we should take a break. From each other."

Rob didn't move. He didn't open his eyes. He didn't say a word.

Holly picked a blade of grass and nibbled it. What was he thinking? Was he about to leap to his feet and beg her to stay? Sit up and start crying? Calmly tell her he felt the same way?

"Rob? Did you hear me?"

He opened his eyes at last. "Yeah. Sure, I heard you." He sat up and took a sip of iced tea.

That was it? Was that his reaction?

"So, what do you think?" Holly asked.

"Um, sure, whatever you want," Rob said. "Sounds okay to me."

This was too easy. She never expected him to be so cool about it. Frankly, she thought he liked her more than that.

"So we're agreed?" she asked.

"Agreed." Rob said. He started gathering up the picnic things. "Great picnic, Holly. I'm stuffed."

"Thanks." This was almost weird. What was he, some kind of heartless Stepford boy?

He helped Holly fold up the blanket and they walked to his SUV. "I'm going to have to go for a run later," Rob said. "Or I'll be floating like a beached whale at swim practice tomorrow."

They loaded up the car and he drove her home. By now it was early evening. He sure was taking the breakup well. It was almost too good to be true.

They pulled up in front of Holly's house. Rob got out and opened the back so Holly could get her picnic basket.

"Thanks again for the picnic," he said. "Mind?"

He leaned close and kissed her. She was used to kissing him, so it didn't surprise her at first. But in the middle of it she thought, *Better enjoy this, because it may be your last Rob kiss.*

When it was over, she stood on the sidewalk for a few seconds, waiting for something to happen. He smiled and got back in the SUV. "See you tomorrow," he said. "Want to catch a movie or something this weekend?"

What? Catch a movie? Wasn't he taking this breakup thing a little too casually?

"Um, I can't," Holly said. "I promised Lina and Mads—"

"No problem," Rob said. "I'll call you later."

She clutched her picnic basket as he drove away. Exactly what was going on here? Hadn't she just broken up with him? Why did he seem to be completely unaware of it? How clueless could he be?

8 Badminton Smackdown!

| To: linaonme |
| From: your daily horoscope |

HERE IS TODAY'S HOROSCOPE: CANCER: I look in my crystal ball and see . . . another crystal ball. That's weird. You figure it out.

Dear Lara,

How was your day today? Seen any good movies lately? Ha ha. I look forward so much to hearing from you every evening. Especially after a bad day, your e-mails really brighten things up.

Did your professor like your paper on Latvian animation? I have to admit I've never seen any Latvian films, so I don't know much about it other than what you wrote me, but it sounds fascinating. I had no idea that *Gilmore Girls* was based on Latvian folktales.

Today was one of those days where I wanted to walk out and quit teaching forever. One of my tenth-graders did an extra credit report (his midterm project was so hopeless I had to give him the chance to make it up with extra credit or he'd fail, god forbid) on a book he apparently found on his mother's night table called *Erotic Fantasies for Women*. I stopped him before he'd read too much out loud but it seems that every boy in the class has already memorized the whole book. They kept asking me leading questions about what they should do if a cute, shirtless handyman wants to come in and wash up or the pool guy wants to take a dip. It was a nightmare. I wonder if I should talk to the kid's parents but I'd have to go through "Rod" first, and I don't think I can take another half-hour lecture on the paradigms for empowering students to leverage their developmentally-appropriate higher-order thinking.

Sorry for going on and on about school—you must find it boring, but it feels good to have someone to vent the day's frustrations to. Write back and tell me all about your day. I love to hear about your world—it takes me away from my own dreary reality. I know you have your difficulties but you handle them so gracefully.

—Beau

Lina was hooked on Dan's e-mails like a hyperactive kid on sugar. They wrote at least once a day now. When Holly and Mads asked her about it, she told them the e-mails were petering out. She just couldn't share it with them anymore—not if Holly and Mads were going to make fun of them. And Lina knew they would. She couldn't bear that. The e-mails meant too much to her.

She could tell he was hooked on them, too, and that made her pulse race. She always knew he'd like her if he let himself get to know her—and she was right. She had proof. He clearly liked and admired her, or "Larissa," any-way, and Lina thought she sensed a romance budding between the lines. He wanted to ask Larissa out, she knew he did. If Larissa gave him the tiniest crumb of encour-agement, he'd snatch it up. But without her encourage-ment he was shy. Maybe she had made Larissa a little too glamorous. She had the feeling he was intimidated by her.

But that glamour was Lina's disguise, and she wasn't ready to drop it yet. Besides, she loved being Larissa, going to gallery openings and movie screenings and bistro dinners with visiting filmmakers. No wonder Dan had stars in his eyes. Lina did, too.

Meanwhile, back in "dreary reality," Lina had been in the class Dan described, where Karl Levine tried to read from his mother's book. She'd seen the discomfort on

Dan's face and felt terrible for him, but the boys just
wouldn't let up. It was as if some bug had gotten inside
them, all at once, and nothing would calm them down.
But it felt so strange to come home and read about it in
Dan's e-mail. He played it cool in class, but the problems
that came up bothered him more than she'd realized.

Hello Beau,

I'm so sorry you had a bad day. Don't let your students get to
you. I'm sure they like and respect you. But sometimes
one boy starts trouble and it snowballs, and even the
greatest teacher in the world wouldn't be able to stop it.
It happened lots of times when I was in high school.

I had a frustrating day today, too. I really wanted to take a
seminar called "Freddy Prinze, Jr.: From Shaggy to
Shakespeare," but the class was full before I had a
chance to sign up. And Professor Stockhauser said he
hasn't had a chance to read my Latvian animation paper
yet. And a friend of mine is having a big party, but I have
too much reading to do and can't go.

I hope you have a better day tomorrow. Maybe you should
watch a movie tonight. I know that always takes my
mind off my troubles, at least for a little while. Why do
you think I'm going to film school?

—Lara

Where is this going? she wondered as she sent her e-mail off to him. How would it end? She could hardly stand to think about it—yet she couldn't stop thinking about it.

"Can't anybody in this school write a decent poem?" Ramona complained. Lina sat in the *Inchworm* office with her and the other members of the Dan Shulman Cult, Siobhan Gallagher, Maggie Schwartzman, and Chandra Bledsoe. Together they made up the entire editorial staff of the magazine, except for Dan Shulman, Faculty Advisor. Ramona had invited Lina to sit in with them and read through some submissions.

Ramona and her friends all wore thin ties of various patterns knotted around their necks. It was their cult symbol, indicating their worship of Dan. Lina hated the ties at first, but they were beginning to grow on her. Still, she'd never wear one herself. It was too stupid. She wondered if Dan had noticed them yet, and if so, what he thought it was supposed to mean. She wished she could ask him about it in an e-mail.

"Listen to this," Ramona said, tapping her ghostly white cheek with a green glittery nail. "'Keith Carter's Wild Ride. I'm Keith Carter, that's my name, I ride my motorbike to national fame—'"

"Ugh. Reject," Chandra said. She'd drawn a tiny

pentagram between her eyes in red ink.

"Here's a good one." Siobhan held up a piece of torn notebook paper covered in purple scrawl. "'My so-called best friend/has abandoned me/she left a hole in me that hurts/like an infected tongue piercing/crusted over—'"

"Gross," Lina said.

"But vivid," Ramona said. "Put it in the maybe pile."

"So far we have two maybes, tons of nos, and five yeses, all of which were written by us," Maggie said.

"If we don't get enough material, we won't publish this issue," Ramona said. "I won't publish motorbike epics just because we don't have anything better." She glanced at Lina. "You're quiet today."

Lina shrugged. "I'm just listening and learning from the pros."

"Sure," Ramona said. "I know you. You think we're idiots. There must be something else on your mind."

Lina stretched her mouth into the most convincing smile she could muster. "No, really. Nothing on my mind. See? Empty." She knocked on her head for emphasis. Ramona would die if she knew about "Beauregard." An accidental discovery like the one Lina had made was the Holy Grail for the Cult, second only to getting Dan to profess his love for one or more of them. To this end they cast numerous spells on him and performed ceremonies and rituals meant to capture his heart, with meager results. Certainly nothing to rival a full-fledged, intimate e-mail correspondence with Dan.

Sometimes Lina was tempted to tell Ramona about it. She knew Ramona would understand in a way that Holly and Mads never could. Holly and Mads thought that writing to Beauregard was funny, a kick. But to Lina it was almost like a real love affair, and Ramona was the only other person in the world who could appreciate it.

But Lina knew she couldn't tell Ramona. She couldn't trust Ramona not to give her away, for one thing. After all, Ramona loved Dan, too, and she might get jealous.

"Does Dan ever have a say in which poems you publish?" Lina asked. "I mean, he's a guy. Maybe he likes motorbike epics."

Ramona made a face. "Are you crazy? Dan likes what we like."

"How do you know?" Lina asked.

"We know," Ramona said.

"We can see him in our crystal ball," Maggie said. She jolted in her seat as Ramona kicked her under the table. "What? Well, Ramona can, anyway."

"Crystal ball?" Lina asked.

"Well, we're *trying* to see him," Ramona admitted. "We have a crystal ball, and we look into it. Sometimes I swear

I see him riding his bike or buying coffee."

Lina glanced at the other girls, who wouldn't meet her eye. Nobody saw any such thing, she knew. But they were all going along with it, humoring Ramona.

"You should come to the museum this Friday," Chandra said. "It's ritual night."

"Let me guess," Lina said. "You cast spells on each other to turn your hair unnatural colors?"

"I'll let that go," Ramona said. "Because I know that somewhere in your future there's a bottle of magenta hair dye waiting. And when that day comes, when you realize you're really a magenta-head at heart, you'll look back on the silly comments you made to us and feel a pang of regret."

Over hair dye? Talk about over-dramatizing.

"On ritual night we perform the SDLC," Chandra said. Off Lina's blank look she added, "The Sacred Dan Love Ceremony."

"Don't tell her about it, Chandra," Ramona said. "She doesn't care about that stuff."

Lina wanted to pretend she didn't care, but she was curious.

"We take one of his artifacts . . . " Chandra said. The Cult collected Dan memorabilia such as used coffee cups, uneaten pizza crusts, and stray hairs to put on display in the "museum." "We put it on the altar, light it on fire, and chant 'See the light as it burns, See the truth in the fire, You have but one love, Chandra, Chandra, She's the one that you desire.' Except each girl puts in her own name in place of Chandra."

"Really?" Lina said. It was even stupider than she'd imagined.

"We're starting to run out of artifacts, though," Maggie said. "We've really got to hit the cafeteria tomorrow. He leaves all kinds of stuff on his tray. Used napkins are the best, because they burn so well."

"That's disgusting," Lina said.

"It's only Dan germs," Maggie said.

"I think it's starting to work," Siobhan said. "You should see what Dan wrote on Ramona's last paper. What did it say again?"

"'Your reading comprehension skills are admirable,'" Maggie recited. "'But of course, I'd expect that from you.'"

"Wow," Lina said. "Book a caterer—I hear wedding bells."

"It's one of those things where you have to read between the lines," Ramona said. "And know what came before. The context. It could be a secret signal. We'll do a handwriting analysis on it this weekend and find out."

"I'd love to come," Lina said. "But I've got some

cuticles that need trimming, and you know how it is—you can't let that go for long. Whoops—that reminds me." She jumped to her feet and gathered her bag. "I've got my first sportswriting gig for the *Seer*." She'd gone to an editorial meeting the day before and received her assignment from Kate Bryson.

"Ooh, the *Seer*," Ramona said in a mocking voice. "And they call that waste of paper news. What are you covering, fifty minutes of testosterone-crazed morons bashing each other with lacrosse sticks?"

"No, I'm covering girls' badminton," Lina said. "I doubt there will be much testosterone or bashing. Now if you don't mind, I've got to go."

"You're hiding something, Ozu," Ramona called as Lina left the room. "You think I don't have powers, but I do. I can tell when something's up, and something's up. But the goddesses will reveal all when it's time for me to know."

Lina hurried down the hall to get away from that goddess talk as fast as she could. And she didn't want to be late for her first sports assignment, even though she'd been disappointed when she found it out was only a bad-minton match, and intramural to boot. In other words, nobody cared about it at all, except maybe the ten girls in the badminton club. And even that was doubtful.

• • •

"Fault!" the referee, Ginnie the Gym Teacher, called. Lina dutifully jotted it in her notebook. "Scintillating match-up between singles players Bridget Aiken and Lulu Ramos. Score: three-love, Aiken. Ramos faults on first serve—probably distracted by tiny cut-off top that rides up every time she lifts her racket."

"Ramos, second serve," Ginny barked. Lulu, chomping on gum, sighed and whacked the shuttlecock into the net.

"Aiken serves," Ginny said. Bridget picked the shuttlecock out of the net and walked pertly to her service corner. Lulu tugged at the bottom of her skirt. She was a tattooed bottle-blond whose naturally dark hair struggled mightily to assert itself against the peroxide. Lina had a strong hunch that Lulu was only taking badminton because RSAGE required students to play at least one sport for three years, and badminton was the easiest. Unlike the perky Bridget, Lulu wasn't the badminton type.

"How's your first assignment going?" Walker sat beside her in the nearly-empty bleachers. "Don't feel bad if this doesn't make the paper. It has nothing to do with your writing—it's just that it's hard to squeeze an exciting story out of intramural badminton. Kate's just trying you out."

"Actually, an interesting angle occurred to me," Lina

said. "Who's on the badminton squad, anyway? What's a girl like Lulu doing here, or Rania Burke, or Abby Kurtz?" Lina nodded toward Rania, a hip-hop diva type, and Abby, a sneering punk rocker covered with so many chains and studs she clanked.

"Sports requirement?" Walker said.

"Exactly. But look what a motley crew it's brought together. The badminton team might be the most diverse squad in the school, socially, and why? Because so many of its members have one thing in common—they hate sports."

"Interesting," Walker said. "The sport for people who hate sports. Except for Bridget over there. And her friend Miriam."

Bridget and Miriam were the only girls in the gym who wore the regulation badminton uniform in the Rosewood colors, white and pink. The rest of the team wore t-shirts, cut-offs, pleather minis—just about anything but appropriate badminton wear. But since it was just an intramural sport and they rarely played teams from other schools, Ginnie didn't waste her energy enforcing the dress code. It was hard enough just to get the team to show up for practice.

"Fault!" Bridget screamed after Lulu finally batted a serve that scored a point. "Her foot went over the line!"

"Who gives a—" Lulu began, but Bridget cut her off,

saying, "Maybe if we were playing in the backseat of a car you'd pay more attention."

"You little—" Lulu ran under the net and dove for Bridget, knocking her to the gym floor. Ginnie blasted her whistle. "Girls! Girls! Stop it right now!"

"Whoa," Walker said. "Lulu just opened up a can of badminton whoop-ass on Bridget. Maybe there is more of a story here than I thought."

Lina snapped a picture of Ginnie breaking up the fight. "We're going to revolutionize the sports page." She scribbled "Badminton Smackdown!" in her notebook.

"Cat fight—I love it. But I've got to go cover the girls' soccer game," Walker said. "I can only hope it will be as exciting. See you later."

"See you," Lina said. Things calmed down in the gym, and Ginnie disqualified Lulu for unsportsmanlike behavior. Game, Set, Match: Bridget.

"Good," Lulu snarled as she stormed out of the gym. "Now I can finally leave this yawn factory."

The next match began. Lina's mind wandered. What would Larissa be doing now? Certainly not sitting in a gym watching girls bat a shuttlecock around. Maybe sitting in a dark movie theater, thinking of Dan.

If only she could be Larissa for real. Wouldn't everything be better then?

9 Portraits

HERE IS TODAY'S HOROSCOPE: VIRGO: The answer to a sticky problem will come to you from an unexpected source.

That's your sister?" Stephen asked. He and Mads were in the art room one afternoon, working on their projects as usual. Mads had taken portrait photos of her mother, father, sister Audrey and brother Adam, who was home from college that week, nerding up the place. Eleven-year-old Audrey, the living Bratz doll, was posed in her signature style—pink Juicy Couture sweatpants, a white t-shirt (cut off at the waist and flashing a pink sequined heart on the front), strawberry-blond hair tied with a pink velvet bow in a high ponytail. She was doing her best Britney imitation, sticking out her lower lip (her idea of a pout), hands on hips.

"Is something wrong with her mouth?" Stephen asked.

"No," Mads said. "She's trying to look sexy."

"Looks like a bee stung her lower lip."

"I know. She always poses that way. Do you think I should draw her like that or try to correct it?"

"I guess it depends on which way expresses the true Audrey," Stephen said.

"Definitely lip-out," Mads said.

"Then draw her that way." Stephen flipped through the photos. "That's my dad," Mads said, pointing to a shot of her father sitting at his cluttered desk in his home office. "He's a labor lawyer." Russell Markowitz's graying hair puffed around his head as if it had never known a comb. He grinned from behind his big glasses.

"He looks like a nice guy," Stephen said.

"Yeah. He's so nice we call him the Dark Overlord as a joke."

Stephen flipped to a picture of a slim woman with frizzy blond hair and red cat's-eye glasses, sitting in the lotus position with a Siamese cat on her knee. "Captain Meow-Meow? And Mom, right?"

"We call her M.C.," Mads said. "For Mary Claire. She's a pet shrink. Holistic, of course."

"Is there any other kind?" There was one more picture in the pile. A nineteen-year-old with thick black hair and glasses like his dad, face contorted in pain over a table full of dead plants. "Who's that?"

"That's my brother, Adam," Mads said. "He's about to kill me because he left me in charge of his plants while he's away at college. I watered them maybe once. Basically, I killed them. I tried to warn him—I've got a black thumb. Thumb of death. Not like Adam and M.C. They can make anything grow."

Stephen set the photos on Mads' art table. "These portraits are going to be good," he said. "They all tell a story. But you'd better get to work. You've got a lot of people to immortalize in pastel."

"Look who's talking," Mads said, nodding toward his bedroom installation. "You've still got a whole dresser to build—and fill with clothes."

"How many more portraits are you planning to do?" Stephen asked.

"Well, I've got one more photo to take," Mads said. "Sean Benedetto."

"You're doing a portrait of him?" Stephen asked.

"Sure." Mads smiled. "He kind of cries out to be

immortalized in pastel. Don't you think?"

Stephen shrugged. "It's your art project. How are you going to pose him?"

"I don't know yet," Mads said. "I know my family and Holly and Lina so well, it's easy for me to find ways to express their personalities. But how to show Sean's? He's such a complicated person."

"He is?" Stephen asked.

"Definitely," Mads said.

"I don't know the guy. What kinds of things is he interested in?"

"I don't know," Mads said. "Partying. Music."

Mads went to the window. She could see the school playing fields in the distance. The girls soccer team was running drills, and the boys lacrosse squad broke up for laps.

"Some artists use athletes for inspiration," Stephen said. "Degas painted dancers—"

"He's a great swimmer," Mads said. "Maybe I'll pose him in his bathing suit."

Stephen laughed. "His bathing suit? Would he do that for you?"

"I don't know," Mads said. But the more she thought about it, the more excited she got. It was perfect. She'd make it the centerpiece of her show. Maybe she could even draw him life-sized!

But Stephen had a point. She could probably get Sean to stop long enough to let her take a snapshot of him in his normal clothes. But how could she get him to pose in his bathing suit?

10 The Awful Truth

HERE IS TODAY'S HOROSCOPE: CAPRICORN: Something confusing will happen today. But you're used to that by now, right?

Have you ever seen the Eleven before?" Mo asked Holly. They leaned against the jukebox at the Rutgers Roadhouse Saturday night, waiting for the Kevin Eleven to take the small wooden stage.

"No, never seen them before," she said.

"You'll like them. They're great to dance to."

Holly watched as kids paid the three-dollar cover

charge and streamed into the bar. The Roadhouse was a low, ramshackle wooden building that had been there forever. They served pizza and burgers and beer; bands played there most nights. This was an all-ages show. Anyone could come in but you needed to show ID to get a beer.

Holly recognized a few kids from school. Sean, with his leggy blond friend Jane, nodded at Mo from across the bar. Holly realized that she'd been seeing Sean at social events with Jane for several weeks in a row now. That went against the usual Sean pattern of a new girl every week. Holly wondered if Mads had noticed it, too. It was a new development, and not good for Mads' chances. Not if Sean and Jane were getting serious.

Then Autumn breezed in, trailed by Vince, Rebecca, and David. Autumn stuck her hand in the back pocket of Vince's jeans, and Vince did the same. They marched around the room, stopping for a long, showy kiss every few feet. Autumn was soaking it up. She couldn't get enough attention, but then everybody already knew that. Vince was the surprise. He grinned like a movie star at people he didn't even know. Holly had thought he was quiet and shy. She'd thought he might calm Autumn down. But it seemed that the opposite had happened— Autumn had hyped him up. They were hanging all over each other. A slow song came on the jukebox and Autumn immediately pressed herself against Vince. They swayed and kissed, even though no one else in the room was dancing. They obviously didn't mind—people who weren't dancing had more time to stare at Autumn and Vince and be jealous of their passion.

"Uh, you fixed those two up, didn't you?" Mo said.

Holly nodded. "I think I've created a monster."

"I'll say. They're grossing me way the hell out."

In her mind, Holly started writing a new quiz. Some people needed to learn about how to behave in public.

Are You a PDA-aholic?

Do you and your honey gross everyone out with your constant Public Displays of Affection? Take this quiz and find out if you need to tone it down! Grade each statement with a 1 (not like you at all), 2 (sort of like you), or 3 (so like you it's scary).

1. ▶ Your idea of a polite greeting is full-body contact.

2. ▶ You spend so much time lip-locked you're not even sure what your honey looks like.

3. ▶ You're always the last to leave a party—you come up for air and everybody's gone.

4. ▶ When people see the two of you coming, they reach for their rain slickers and umbrellas.

5. ▶ You know what your boyfriend ate for breakfast without his having to tell you.
6. ▶ You brush your teeth before you call your honey just in case she can smell your breath over the phone.
7. ▶ You're covered with so many hickeys people call you "Redneck."

If you scored 7-10 points: COLD FISH. You do not have a PDA problem. You could probably stand to loosen up a little. Your honey is starving for affection!

If you scored 11-16 points: NORMAL LOVEBIRDS. You're affectionate without being icky. You have each other; you don't have to drag everyone else into it.

If you scored 17-21 points: BLECH! Keep it under wraps, would you? Who are you trying to impress?

The Kevin Eleven finally jumped onstage. The crowd hooted. "Hey," Holly said to Mo. "There are only four of them. Not eleven."

"That's part of the joke," Mo said. "I think they just like the way the name rhymes."

"Is there someone on that stage named Kevin, at least?" Holly asked.

"Actually . . . no. The lead singer's name is Cyrus."

The band played a country-tinged rock song and

people started dancing. Mo took Holly's hand and they bopped from side to side together. Autumn and Vince were still glued to each other, even though this wasn't a slow dance.

Mo awkwardly twirled Holly around, and she saw the door open. A tall, broad-shouldered boy with choppy brown hair walked in. He wore a red t-shirt that said, I'M OUT OF BED—WHAT MORE DO YOU WANT?

Oh no. It wasn't . . . Yes, it was. Rob.

He spotted her, waved, and worked his way through the crowd toward her and Mo. Mo hadn't noticed him yet and didn't realize that trouble was headed his way. Holly, on the other hand, was acutely aware of it.

"Hey!" Rob said. He kissed Holly on the cheek as if she were still his girlfriend. "Lucky to find you here. How's it going, Mo?"

Mo stared at him for a minute, clearly confused. "It's going fine," he said slowly. "I guess."

Rob took Holly's free hand and danced a few steps with her. Then he said, "Let's get something to drink. Mo, you want something?"

"I'm fine," Holly said.

"Me, too," Mo said.

"Sure? Okay. I'll go get a Red Bull." Rob drifted over to the bar.

"Holly, what the hell is going on?" Mo asked. "I thought you broke up with him."

"I did," Holly said. "You should have heard me. I'm not sure *he* heard me, though."

"Well, I don't think he has any idea what's going on here," Mo said. "He doesn't seem to realize we're on a date. You want me to talk to him?"

It was tempting, but Holly knew she had to do it herself. "No, thanks, Mo. I'll talk to him. I'm sorry about this." Rob had gotten his drink and was headed back toward them. "I'll take care of it right now. Wait here."

She intercepted Rob. "Hey, can we go outside for a minute?" she said.

"Sure. Whatever you want." Rob followed her out the door. They stood in the light of a street lamp illuminating the roadhouse parking lot.

"What's up?" Rob said. "Haven't talked to you in a few days."

"I know," Holly said. "That's what usually happens when you break up with someone."

He half-laughed. "Quit kidding around, Holly. Let's go back inside and dance."

"Rob, please," Holly said. "You have to listen to me." She stared at the t-shirt for extra motivation. *Keep your eyes on the shirt,* she told herself. *Always on the shirt . . .*

"Holly, you've been really weird ever since that picnic," Rob said.

"Yes," Holly said. "The picnic. Don't you remember what I said at the picnic?"

"Um . . . not really. I didn't know there was going to be a test."

Holly frowned, frustrated. It was hard enough to break up with him the first time. Why was he making her do it again?

"Holly, if you want to say something, just say it. Like you usually do. Grinchy." He grinned to show he was just teasing.

"You don't remember anything?" Holly asked. "Like I thought we needed some space? And should see other people? In other words, break up?"

He looked stunned. Why was he doing this? Was he just playing dumb to avoid a real breakup? Or did he really not get what she was trying to say?

"Break up?" he said. "Why?"

"It's nothing big. You're a great guy. But all these little things—"

"Like what? Tell me. I really want to know."

"Okay. The way you ask permission before you kiss me? That drives me nuts. And the way you always say you want to do whatever I want, and never express your own opinion? I mean, I can't believe we sat through a whole lunch at Phony Baloney and you never said a word!"

"What would be the point?" Rob said. "I was trying to make the best of a bad situation."

"*I* had to say something—" Holly began.

"You're the one who wanted to go there in the first place," Rob said. "Why did you take me there if you don't like it? I don't get you."

"I was trying to teach you a lesson!"

"A lesson? About what?"

"About speaking up for yourself!"

"Thanks a lot. I really need lessons from you, the Phony Baloney Love Ninja!"

Ooh, he was asking for it now. "Why don't you put it on a t-shirt? You'll say anything if it's printed on a cotton-poly blend!"

His face went slack, then pale. She'd finally gotten through to him—Holly could see that now. But the look on his face . . . it pierced her heart. She'd tried so hard to avoid hurting him, and look what happened. She'd blurted out everything in the meanest way possible. She wished she could take it all back now, every word.

"You know, for somebody who's good at speaking her mind, you sure kept a lot of grievances bottled up," Rob said. "I'm out of here." He turned and started toward his SUV. Then he stopped.

"Holly, I have a confession to make. When we were at the picnic, and I was lying down after we ate, and you were talking to me? Well, I fell asleep. Just for a few minutes. But I guess I missed the part where you said you wanted to break up. And I didn't want to upset you and admit that I fell asleep, so I just pretended to go along with whatever it was you were saying. Now I know what I missed. It was bigger than I thought."

He climbed into the car and drove off. Holly watched him peel out. Now *she* was the one who was stunned. He was *asleep?* He never heard her? So he wasn't clueless after all. Just too chicken to tell her that he fell asleep while she was talking. Well, wasn't that part of the problem? If only he'd said something then, none of this would have happened.

He wasn't afraid to speak his mind anymore. That was clear.

11 Lina Slips Up

HERE IS TODAY'S HOROSCOPE: CANCER: You're swimming in shark-infested waters with a bleeding cut on your knee. You know what that means, don't you? CHOMP!

Lina walked down the hall that dead-ended at the *Inchworm* office. Kate Bryson had liked Lina's badminton story so much she made it the top sports headline, ahead of the big swim team victory. Then she loaded up Lina with assignments. Lina had decided she didn't have time to work on *Inchworm* anymore—she'd concentrate on the *Seer* instead. But she had to break it to Ramona, who, she knew, probably wouldn't much care.

She heard no cackling or soaring pronouncements from the hall, which meant that Ramona and the cult were probably not there. She peeked into the office. Dan sat at a desk reading Ramona's latest recommendations for publication. He looked up when Lina popped her head in.

"Hey, Lina," he said. "What can I do for you?"

Her heart started pounding, as it always did when she was alone with him. "I was just looking for Ramona."

"Not here," he said. "I saw your article in the *Seer* this morning. Nice work. I'm not a big badminton fan but you'll find me in the stands at the next match. Along with a lot of other spectators, I bet. Who knew badminton could be so dramatic?"

Lina wasn't sure whether to laugh or nod or say something smart, which was impossible since her brain was frozen, so she just shrugged. *Beauregard, it's me, Larissa,* she thought as she noticed for the millionth time how sincere his blue eyes looked, even when he was joking. *Can't you tell it's me?*

He grinned at her. He definitely couldn't tell. He was way too relaxed. To him this was just an everyday student-teacher encounter.

"Dan, there you are." John Alvarado, the principal, appeared in the doorway behind Lina, startling her. "Hello, Lina."

"Hi."

"Listen, Dan, we're having a mission-critical interface tomorrow to recontextualize our action plans for the CRT. We'll be discussing the principles of Total Quality Management, so if you haven't read the printout I left in your box, now's the time. Just a heads-up."

Lina thought she caught a hint of amusement flash across Dan's face, but she couldn't be sure. He nodded soberly and said, "No problem. I'll be there."

"Great. See you at the interface. Happy educating."

"Same to you," Dan said when Mr. Alvarado had left.

Lina snickered. "Later, Rod." Then she froze. Oh no. Rod. Dan's nickname for Mr. Alvarado. He and Mlle. Barker—and Larissa—were the only ones who knew about it!

She checked Dan for a reaction. Her joke didn't seem to have registered. Maybe he didn't hear her. She did say it kind of softly. . . .

"Lina, if I ever start talking like that guy, you have my permission to shoot me," Dan said. "Seriously. Just put me out of my misery."

So was he on to her, or not? Lina couldn't tell. He didn't seem upset, but then he rarely did.

"Uh, it's a deal," she said. "Well, I'd better find Ramona. Guess I'll check the smoking bathroom."

Oops—another slip. The teachers weren't supposed to know there was a smoking bathroom—designated by the "bad girls"—in the basement of the school. But Dan shrugged it off. Maybe the cool teachers were on to it and didn't want to start a fuss.

He went back to his reading. "All right. See you in class."

Lina walked away as fast as she could, her heart racing. That was too close! What if he'd guessed she was Larissa! What if it occurred to him later? What should she do?

There was nothing she could do—but wait. His next e-mail would tell the tale.

Dear Lara,

Another tough day. The chain on my bike broke as I was riding to school this morning. I had to walk my bike home, clean off the grease that had gotten all over my hands and my pants, change, and take the car to school. Of course I was late. And that was only the beginning.

But things brightened up as the school day drew to an end and every minute brought me closer to another e-mail from you. You have no idea how much our correspondence means to me. It struck me tonight as I stopped at the market to get some things for supper. I was humming, I bought flowers—I felt as if I was cooking for someone special tonight. In reality it was only me and the neighbor's cat, who likes to drop by around supper-time every evening. But I felt another presence at the table. And it was yours. I didn't feel alone, knowing that after I washed the dishes I'd sit down at my laptop and write to you again.

I hope you won't think this is forward of me, but with every day that passes I get more and more curious about you. Every aspect of you interests me. And I can't help wondering—what do you look like? You saw my photo in my ad on The List. If you were so inclined, I'd love to see yours. Could you send one to me? Only if you feel comfortable about it, of course. I'm interested in everything about you, not just how you look.

Well, dear Lara, milaya Lara, as they say in Russian (I asked a friend), I wish you another good night, another peaceful sleep.

Your Beau

I'm going to swoon, Lina thought, feeling dizzy with excitement. *For the first time in my life I understand what the word "swoon" really means.*

His e-mails got better every day. This was the best one yet.

He's crazy about me! Lina thought. *I mean, about her. Oh, I don't know what I mean!*

He hadn't said anything about Rod, or Mr. Alvarado, or how weird it was that a student knew his secret nickname for the principal. *Maybe he didn't notice,* Lina thought. *Maybe he didn't care.*

Anyway, it looked as if she'd gotten away with it. But it was too easy to let those little things slip out. She was going to have to be more careful from now on if she didn't want to be discovered.

But she had a new problem. He wanted to see a picture! She should have known this would come up eventually. What was she going to do?

She would ignore it, she decided. She'd just ignore his first request for a photo. And if he asked again, she'd make something up. Or find a picture of somebody else, maybe a friend of Piper's, that she could send instead. She'd worry about that later. Maybe he wouldn't press her about it. He seemed very sensitive to the possibility that she might not want to send pictures of herself to just anybody on the Internet. And that was perfectly reasonable. Except that her e-mails to him—like his to her—were more and more intimate, and sending a picture seemed natural at this point.

She wished she could tell him the truth when she saw

him at school. She wished that would make everything okay.

But she knew that telling him the truth could ruin the whole thing. And she wasn't ready to lose her Beau. Not yet.

12 All's Fair in Love and Art

HERE IS TODAY'S HOROSCOPE: VIRGO: There's a fine line between clever and kooky, and you crossed over to the kooky side long ago.

Mads had a plan. She pulled Lina into the Swim Center Wednesday afternoon. The pool was lively with shouts, whistles, and splashes, the sounds of both the boys and girls swim teams practicing.

"Mads, this is against all the ethics of journalism," Lina protested, dragging her feet.

"Don't think of it as journalism," Mads said. "This isn't

about journalism. It's about love! And art. And all's fair in love and war, and I'm sure that goes for art, too. You should know. You're a poet."

"I guess . . ."

"Anyway, you can ask him real questions if you want. You might actually get a story out of this," Mads said.

"I don't really see a good angle here," Lina said. "Although 'Sophomore Tricks Hunk into Posing for Sexy Photo' might make a nice headline."

"Come on, Lina," Mads said. "Don't pull journalistic standards on me now. Remember a little piece called 'Badminton Smackdown'?"

"Well, I guess it won't hurt anyone—"

"Exactly. Come on, there's Sean."

Sean had just emerged from the boys' locker room, adjusting his goggles. Mads loved to see him in his bathing suit. He was lean and muscular but not too bulked up, and even with his shaggy blond hair tucked under a swim cap, he still looked cool. The cap only made you notice more than ever what a great face he had.

Mads and Lina crossed the bleachers toward him. Before they reached him a whistle blew, and Rob pulled himself out of the pool and stood in front of them, dripping. Awkward. Way awkward.

"Hi, Rob," Mads said. She still liked him even though

Holly had dumped him. Both Mads and Lina thought Holly was crazy.

He wasn't wearing his cap and his thick, choppy hair clumped up when wet. He looked like a puppy who'd just gotten a bath. "Hi," he said. "What are you doing here?"

"We're on a mission," Mads said. "Uh, of a journalistic nature."

"That's cool. How's Holly doing?"

"How's Holly doing?" Mads echoed. "Um, I don't know. How's she doing, Lina?"

"She's okay," Lina said. The truth was, Holly felt bad about the way she'd left things with Rob at the Rutgers Roadhouse. Mads and Lina heard all about it the next day. But Holly was convinced it was for the best. She was just sorry about the way things happened. Rob probably wouldn't want to be friends with her for a while, if ever.

"Should we tell her you said hello?" Mads asked.

"No," Rob said. "Don't tell her I said anything."

The coach shouted, "Back in the pool, Safran! Breaststroke!" Rob dove in and swam away.

"Come on, let's catch Sean before the coach nabs him," Mads said. "You know the plan."

They stopped Sean before he reached the pool. "Hey girls," he said. "What's shaking?"

Mads elbowed Lina. "I'm, hi, Sean, I don't know if you

know me, I'm Lina Ozu, and I'm a sports reporter for the *Seer*."

"Sure, I've seen you around," Sean said. "Hey, kid," he added to Mads.

Sean had called Mads "Kid" ever since he first realized she existed—which took a while. At first it bothered her that he couldn't seem to remember her actual name. But she decided to like it. It was kind of cute.

"We're doing a special feature on the swim team," Lina said. "Do you have a few minutes for an interview?"

"Sure, no worries." Sean crossed his arms. "Ask away." The coach spotted him, blew his whistle, and called, "Benedetto, hit the pool now!"

No! Mads didn't want to lose him so soon. She hadn't even gotten a single shot yet. But she shouldn't have worried. Leave it to Sean.

"This is important, Coach," Sean called back. "I'll be right there."

To Mads' amazement, the coach let it go.

"Um, Sean, I'm taking pictures for the paper," Mads said. "You don't mind, do you? It really helps the story if there's a good visual with it. Right, Lina?"

"Right," Lina said. She struggled to come up with a realistic-sounding question. "Um, so how did you get started swimming?"

"Well, like anybody else, my mother made me take

lessons when I was little—"

Mads swarmed around him like a fly, shooting him from different angles. Sean seemed very aware of the camera. His eyes followed it even as he talked.

"Sean, can I get one with your hands on your hips?" Mads asked. Sean hesitated, but Lina distracted him with, "So now you're the star swimmer on the team, wouldn't you say?"

Sean struck the pose Mads had asked for. "We're a team first, individuals second. That's what the coach says, anyway. The team is the star of the team. Wait. Does that make sense?"

Lina nodded. "Uh-huh. Sure."

"Can you flex your muscles, Sean?" Mads asked, snapping away with her digital camera. She stopped to demonstrate the pose she wanted: both arms out to the side, hands balled in fists, biceps flexed. Like Popeye after he's eaten his spinach.

Sean took the Popeye pose, then added a Mr. Universe twist without even being asked. He began to ignore Lina's questions and play more and more to the camera—and right into Mads' hands. He put his goggles over his eyes and made a pro-wrestler face. He took off his swim cap and shook out his hair. He raised his arms over his head like a champion.

"I have a question for you," Mads said. "I'm having a party in a couple of weeks, right after the Art Fair. It's like a post-show party. Can you come? You can bring as many friends as you want."

"After the Art Fair?" Sean paused in his posing to scan the crowded social schedule in his mind. "That's a Friday, right?"

"Right," Mads said. "It's going to be a great party."

"Sounds cool, but I can't. Alex is having a party that night, too," Sean said. "I promised him I'd be there. You know how it is. Gotta support my peeps."

Mads almost dropped her camera. Alex Sipress was having a party the same night as hers? Alex was a senior and almost as popular as Sean. His party would drain all the cool people away from hers. There was no chance any cool people would come. Even the less-cool kids would choose Alex's over Mads', if they had the option. Her big post-Art Fair celebration would be the loser party of the year.

"I think I've got what I need," Mads said. The news about Alex's party had temporarily dampened her enthusiasm for photography. She had plenty of good shots, anyway.

"Great," Lina said. "Thanks for the interview, Sean."

"But you didn't really ask me much," Sean said. "Can you get a whole story out of that? You never even asked about my win in the 300-meter freestyle last week. And what about all my summers on the country club team?"

"I'll call you if I need more information," Lina said. She pinched Mads and whispered, "Come on, let's get out of here."

The coach blew his whistle again and yelled, "Benedetto, are you ready to get your pretty little face wet yet? Get the hell in the water!"

"Later, girls." Sean padded across the cement. He stopped at the edge of the pool and turned around. "When's the story coming out?"

"Um, soon," Lina said. "We'll let you know."

"Cool." He dove into the water. Mads and Lina hurried out of the Swim Center.

"I might as well cancel my party right now," Mads said. "Nobody will come.!"

"I'll be there," Lina said. "And Holly. And all your other friends."

"And you'll be wishing you were at Alex's the whole time," Mads said. "I know I will be. We'll miss all the action!"

"Mads, calm down. There's room for more than one party in this town."

"No, there isn't," Mads said. "There aren't enough cool people to go around. The question is, How much of a draw could a party at my house be? Can I bring in the big guns? Can I put asses in the seats?"

"Mads, what are you talking about?"

"This is a true test of my social power, Lina," Mads said. She couldn't win. And she knew it.

13 Crisis on Rutgers Street

HERE IS TODAY'S HOROSCOPE: CAPRICORN: Wear rubber-soled shoes—today will bring a shock.

Do you think Barton Mitchell is cute?" Holly asked. She and Lina and Mads were coming out of a shop on Rutgers Street and heading for dinner at Ruby's, a café down the block. Mads and Lina had met her for a little shopping after the Sean photo session.

"Why?" Mads asked. "What's wrong with Mo?"

"Nothing's wrong with him, exactly," Holly said. "We've only been out together once. I don't know if he's boyfriend material, though. Have you ever noticed how he sucks his teeth? Like this." Holly put her tongue over her front teeth and made a squeaky sucking sound. "Not all the time. But it's not the kind of thing you like to hear, even once in a while."

Mads and Lina rolled their eyes at each other. "I saw that," Holly said. "I know you guys think I'm too picky. But I'm actually being thoughtful. I don't want to get all tangled up with a guy if he's not right, only to hurt him later. That makes sense, doesn't it?"

"It makes sense in a way," Lina said. "But how can you tell how you really feel about someone unless you get all tangled up with him? Everybody's got irritating habits. If you let that stop you, you'll never find anybody you like."

They were coming up on the Carlton Bay Twin movie theater. One thing Holly liked about Carlton Bay was that it had no malls and no cineplexes. There was a big mall not too far out of town with a twelve-screen theater, but the old Carlton Bay Twin was still running right there on Rutgers Street, as it had been since the 1950s.

The doors opened and people poured into the street. It was just before six, and the late afternoon show had just ended. Holly, Lina, and Mads wove through the crowd milling on the sidewalk.

"We'd better get to Ruby's before this crowd does,"

Holly said. Ruby's was a favorite post-movie spot.

A couple exited the theater just ahead of them and started down the street. The boy had a familiar head of choppy brown hair. He wore a t-shirt that said HUG A LOGGER—YOU'LL NEVER GO BACK TO TREES.

Holly stopped in her tracks and grabbed each of her friends by the arm. "It's Rob."

And he was with a girl. Christie Hubbard, a freshman. They walked down the sidewalk in front of Holly, Lina, and Mads. Rob hadn't seen them. Christie said something to him, and he laughed.

"What is he doing with *her*?" Holly cried. Her blood was speeding through her veins. She was surprised at her own reaction, but the minute she saw Rob she thought, *He's mine.* A fury of possessiveness seized her. Rob walking down the street with another girl—it was just wrong.

"Maybe they're friends," Lina said.

"She's probably a lesbian," Mads said.

Holly squinted at Christie. She was a big-boned girl with curly blond hair, dressed in a full-skirted sundress. A lesbian? Wouldn't that be a little too convenient? "Mads, don't patronize me."

"Okay, calm down, Holly," Lina said. "She probably asked Rob to go to a movie, you know, in that naïve freshman girl way, and he didn't want to hurt her feelings,

121

and anyway, *you* just dumped him, so—"

"Lina, you're not making me feel better," Holly said.

"She's just trying to tell you not to panic," Mads said. "You don't know that there's anything to worry about yet."

But as soon as the words came out of her mouth, Christie gave them something to worry about. Something very definite. A crystal clear signal.

She threw her arms around Rob and gave him a big, wet kiss. And he didn't stop her. In fact, he seemed to like it.

Holly froze. Every organ in her body turned to ice. No. It couldn't be. How could he be kissing another girl?

"Oh. My. God," Mads gasped.

"I don't believe it," Holly said. "He has another girl-friend? Already?"

Rob and Christie broke apart, nuzzled noses, then kissed again. Holly pressed herself against the wall of the movie theater so they wouldn't see her, in case they turned around. But there didn't seem to be much danger of that. They were in a world of their own.

Rob and Christie started down the street again, hand in hand. Tears welled up in Holly's eyes. Her own reaction shocked her. She'd had no idea she felt so attached to Rob.

"Holly? Are you okay?" Lina asked.

"Why are you so upset?" Mads said. "I thought you didn't like him anymore."

"I was wrong," Holly said. "I made a mistake. A big mistake. I want Rob back."

And that's how you know if he's "it," Holly realized. *When it breaks your heart to see him with someone else.*

14 A Proposition

To: linaonme
From: your daily horoscope

HERE IS TODAY'S HOROSCOPE: CANCER: When did you become such a big risk-taker, Cancer? I miss the scaredy-cat you used to be. Bet you'll be back to hiding under the covers soon.

Dear Lara,

So, you're working on your first screenplay! Very exciting! You must be flattered that Steven Spielberg asked you to let him read it. How far along have you gotten? What's it about? I'd love to read it when you're finished, if that's okay. You're so lucky to be so talented and doing what you love. You'll be famous by the time you're thirty, I bet.

Maybe even twenty-five!

Things are chugging along slowly here. I just got out of an endless teachers' meeting about some big new test the State of California is inflicting on us. That Rod sure knows how to talk on and on about nothing. Camille passed me a note that said, "Good thing I've got life insurance because Rod is boring me to death." Her notes are the only thing that keep me from dozing off in those meetings.

I understand why you haven't sent me your picture yet. At least I think I do. But that makes my next request all the more difficult. I hope you won't feel pressured by this. But Lara, Larissa, I'd really love to meet you in person. I can tell from the way we write to each other that we'd talk for hours, so easily, and at the very least we could be effortless friends. No pressure—you're completely free to say no, of course, and if you do I'll still be thrilled just to know you online, as a virtual friend. But if you're curious about me and are feeling brave, here's what I propose: Meet me for lunch. You pick the place, some- where you feel comfortable. I'd be glad to come into the city and meet you somewhere. What do you think? We've been writing to each other for weeks now. To me it feels right. But you do what's best for you. I promise I'll understand, whatever you decide.

> Well, guess I'd better get back to grading papers. These days
> I seem to live from e-mail to e-mail; you are more real
> to me than anything else in my life right now. Good
> night, Larissa. I'll see you in my dreams . . . Beau

Once Lina recovered from her nightly Beauregard swoon, she started to panic. This was it. The chance she'd been waiting for—and terrified of.

She'd ignored the request for a photo, and he'd never repeated it. She thought she was getting away with something. But now he wanted to meet her. And she wanted to have lunch with him more than anything. Imagine sitting at a table with him, looking into his eyes, being on a real date with him at last! But how could she do it? What would he do when he saw her and understood the truth?

This was serious. Ultra-serious. Now more than ever she had to keep the whole Beau thing secret, even from Holly and Mads. Especially if she met him for lunch. Oh god, should she do it? She was dying to go. How could she live with herself, after all she'd been through with him, if she never found out what would happen? Now that he'd seen how mature she could be—she'd been impersonating a grad student, after all—and he was half in love with her, maybe he'd finally understand that they were really meant for each other. Age didn't matter. The difference between them wasn't even that huge. Ten years—nothing! If he were ninety and she were eighty, nobody would bat an eyelash.

All right, she decided. *I'm going to do it. I've got to do it. I have no choice. This is my big chance to get together with the guy I've been dreaming about all year long! How can I let it slip away?*

Then her thoughts turned practical. She had to choose a place to meet. He was expecting to meet her in the city, which was good—the chances of someone they knew spotting them there were small. The trouble was, she didn't know the city *that* well. Where should they meet?

She went online and searched a Web site that listed San Francisco restaurants. Nothing too fancy or expensive—that would turn Dan off. He'd said he didn't want a high-maintenance girl, and Lina wasn't one anyway. But still, she didn't want the biggest moment of her life to take place at some grimy old coffee shop. It had to be romantic.

Then she came across a place that sounded perfect. The Garden Restaurant, with a leafy back garden, moderate prices, and open for lunch, right downtown.

Dear Beauregard,

Thanks for asking about my screenplay. It's going well. I'll tell you all about it when we meet.

Yes, I've decided that you are right—it's time for us to meet. I

know you think I have this glamorous life, but your e-
mails are better than grad school or parties or watching
movies or the best book. I live for them. And I'm very
curious to meet you. I hope you won't be disappointed
when you see me. I don't know what you think I'm like
in person, but I might not be what you expect.

Are you free this Saturday? We could meet at a place I know
downtown called the Garden at one o'clock. If that's all
right with you, just let me know.

Well, I'd better get back to my writing. I can't wait until our
lunch!

Larissa

She re-read it, then pressed SEND. Now all she had
to do was find a way to sneak into the city without anyone knowing. She got up and paced her room. She was
going to have a tough time sleeping that night. At last, a
date with Dan! She'd been dreaming of this moment for
months. What should she wear? Should she do something
with her hair, maybe put it up?

But her happiness was tempered with nervousness,
and even fear. What would happen when he found out the
truth? Would he embrace her? Would he be angry? Would
he give in and realize she was meant for him—or would
she lose him forever?

15 Admirer

> To: mad4u
> From: your daily horoscope
>
> HERE IS TODAY'S HOROSCOPE: VIRGO: You like to meddle,
> don't you? The stars tell me you're going to do it no matter
> what I say, so knock yourself out.

Why are you drawing Stephen's face on Sean's body?" Holly asked Mads. She had come up to the art room to hang out for a few minutes before she went home for the day. The Art Fair was only a week away and Mads was working on her project every afternoon.

"You think it looks like Stephen?" Mads said. "It's not supposed to." She showed Holly the digital beefcake shot of Sean she'd chosen to work from. It was the Popeye, show-me-your-biceps one. Holly burst out laughing.

"You're going to draw him like that? He looks so— so—so—"

"What?" Mads said. "This one had the most interesting composition. The arms give it symmetry but the way he's turned toward the camera adds depth—"

"Who cares about that? What I'm saying is he looks like a cartoon character."

"You think? I don't know. I don't like to judge the picture until it's finished," Mads said. "You never know how it's going to turn out in the end. But I *don't* want his face to look like Stephen's. That's weird." She set the sketch aside. "I'll come back to that one. I think I'll work on you for a while."

"I can't stay long," Holly said. "I've got to go home and sob silently into my pillow."

Mads put down her pastel crayon. She'd seen Rob and Christie earlier that day, holding hands between classes. She wasn't about to tell Holly, though. Holly was a wreck. All she could think about and all she could talk about was Rob. How stupid she was to give him up. How she couldn't believe he found another girlfriend so fast. How she had to find a way to get him to forgive her and take her back, if it wasn't too late.

"Holly, you'll get him back," Mads said. She didn't

know what else to tell her. Why wouldn't Holly get Rob back, or anybody she wanted, for that matter? Holly was ten times prettier, smarter, and cooler than Christie. Mads didn't really know Christie, but it had to be true. "Or you'll get a new guy. A better guy. That was what you wanted in the first place, remember?"

"I know," Holly said.

"And Rob is still wearing those dumb t-shirts," Mads reminded her. "Today he was wearing one that said INSTANT SWIMMER—JUST ADD WATER."

Holly smiled sadly. "That's so adorable."

"That's not what you would have said a few days ago," Mads said.

"Everything seems different now. How long did he wait until he found a new girlfriend? One day?" She paused to take a deep breath. "All right, I'm getting verklempt. I'll get out of here and let you work," Holly said. "IM me when you get home."

"Okay. See you later."

Stephen walked in just as Holly was leaving. "Hi," she said to him.

"Hi," he said. "Going so soon?"

Going so soon? That wasn't something Stephen would normally say. Maybe it was something he said when he had a crush on somebody.

"Got to let the genius do her thing," Holly said. She left, and Stephen walked over to his work area. "Howdy, Mads," he said. "How's it going?"

"Good," she said. She studied the photo of Holly and compared it to what she'd drawn so far. Holly looked so beautiful in the photograph. If only Mads could capture that shiny-eyed, confident quality in her drawing, the portrait of Holly would be one of her best pieces.

She clipped her drawing to the easel and concentrated on Holly's eyes. She was so focused she didn't realize Stephen was watching until he said, "That's a great picture, Mads. Really beautiful."

"Thanks," Mads said.

He picked up the photo to compare with the drawing. "This photograph is beautiful too," he said. "She almost looks Pre-Raphaelite, with all that golden hair."

Pre-Raphaelite? Mads didn't ask. She assumed it was good.

He put the picture down and stared at the drawing some more. "That's going to be a breakthrough for you, Mads. I can tell. Look at the expression in her eyes. It's— it's lovely."

Lovely? Mads watched Stephen's face. Was he talking about the portrait—or about Holly?

Look at the way he's staring at her picture, Mads thought.

She felt a little pinch of disappointment. Why didn't anyone ever look at *her* that way?

He's got a thing for Holly, Mads thought. It was so obvious.

Hmm . . . Maybe it was Mads' turn to play matchmaker for a change. Holly was all twisted up over Rob. But Stephen was a great guy, too. Totally different from Rob, but a fine specimen in his own way. If she could get Holly to forget about Rob and see Stephen the way Mads saw him, she might feel better. And from the way he was drooling over Holly's picture, Mads guessed Stephen would be over the moon.

16 Showdown at the Swim Center

To: hollygolitely
From: your daily horoscope

HERE IS TODAY'S HOROSCOPE: CAPRICORN: You're a tough cookie who doesn't crumble easily. This time, though, I don't like your chances.

Why so glum, my bodacious chum?" Sebastiano asked Holly when she bumped into him at her locker that afternoon. She'd been on a rampage all day, snarling and biting people's heads off if they so much as looked at her wrong. Even Lina and Mads were a little afraid of her. Holly appreciated that Sebastiano saw through her rage to the sadness below.

"You must have seen them around," Holly said. "*I*

can't seem to get away from them."

"You mean Rob and that girl who clings to him like lint on cashmere?" Sebastiano said. "Come on, Holly. You can take her. She's no threat to the Great Boobmeister."

"Oh yeah? Then why is Rob with her and not me?" Holly said. "All I did was tell him we shouldn't date anymore and I wanted to see other people."

Sebastiano patted her shoulder. "There, there. I know it's not fair. But what are you standing here talking to me for? What you need is an all-out assault on the enemy. Don't hint or be subtle. Don't pussyfoot around. Just go right up to him and tell him you want him back. It hasn't been that long—he can't be too attached to the little leech yet. See what happens."

It was blunt, it was simple, it was obvious. It might work. "All right, Sebastiano," she said. "I'll try it this afternoon."

"That's my girl. Who knows, by tonight he could be snuggling up with you again, getting on your nerves and driving you crazy just like the old days." He closed his locker and zipped up his sleek gray sweater.

"Where are you off to?" Holly asked.

"My little sister's ballet recital. No one can accuse me of not supporting the arts. Good luck!"

"Thanks." Holly went to the library to do some

homework and wait out Rob's swim practice. Just before five she left for the Swim Center and staked out the door to the boys' locker room. A few minutes later Rob came out, freshly showered, his messy, wet hair more teddy-bearish than ever.

"Hey." He looked startled to see her. "What are you doing here?"

"Rob, can I talk to you for a minute?" Holly asked.

Rob glanced around. Holly wondered if Christie was supposed to meet him. "Uh, sure."

She led him outside and they settled against a wall near the Swim Center entrance. She took a deep breath. Her instinct was to try to finesse this somehow, but she'd decided to take Sebastiano's advice and just go for it.

"Rob, I was wrong," she said. "Breaking up with you was stupid. A stupid mistake. I must have been in a bad mood that day or something."

"Bad mood, huh? Guess that happens," Rob said.

"I know it's no excuse," Holly said. "Listen, Rob, please. I'd like another chance. A chance to make it up to you and to be together again."

She waited, watching his face carefully for signs of his feelings. It was a mobile face and usually very expressive and easy to read. But that afternoon he kept it stuck in neutral.

"What do you say?" she prompted after he hadn't answered her.

He looked her in the eye now. Ah, good sign. He still liked her, she could see it. And when she looked into his eyes she felt more than ever what a good person he was, how warm and sweet and thoughtful, how perfect for her.

Then he looked down. "No," he said.

No? Did he just say no?

"What do you mean, no?" Holly said. How could he just stand there and say no to her?

"I mean, no, I don't want to get back together with you. I'm sorry."

"But why? We were so good together! You have to admit that."

"I know. But you're not the only one who had things to complain about, you know. I thought you were too critical and too picky. Why did you always have to make such a big deal about little things like what t-shirt I was wearing? All I did was try to be nice to you, and even *that* bugged you! You dumped me, Holly. And why? For the stupidest reasons I ever heard. If you can break up with me that easily, over such petty things, then I don't want to be with you. So I'm sorry, Holly, but the answer is no. I don't want you back. See you."

He hoisted his backpack over his shoulder and

walked away. Holly stared after him, speechless. In all the time she'd known him, which, she had to admit, wasn't all that long, he'd never spoken to her so firmly. Where did it come from?

Reality began to sink in. Holly was devastated. She dropped her head into her hands. She couldn't believe it. He didn't want her back! He just came right out and said so!

Rob was finally standing up for himself. What took him so long?

Thanks a lot, Sebastiano, Holly thought. *Now I feel worse than ever.* Was there really no hope, no way to get him back?

Holly couldn't accept it. *I don't give up so easily,* Holly said to herself. *Christie Hubbard better look out. I'm going to get Rob back if it kills me. Or her. But more likely me.*

17 At Home with Ramona

To:	linaonme
From:	your daily horoscope

HERE IS TODAY'S HOROSCOPE: CANCER: You will experience discomfort today—I mean more than usual.

A nyone sitting here?" Ramona asked.

Lina shook her head. "Sit down."

Mads was busy in the art room every afternoon and Holly had gone to the pool to confront Rob, so Lina, not in the mood to go home yet, had ridden her bike to Vineland by herself. It was not like her to do that. But neither was sneaking into the city alone for a date. Maybe it was time to try new things, be a little bold, come out of her shell.

But when she got to the café, no one she knew was there. She ordered coffee and sat at a table alone, staring out the big picture window at the valley. She was happy to be interrupted by Ramona. Not exactly what you'd call a *friendly* face, but a familiar one at least.

"You must be in a good mood today," Lina said, noting that Ramona had drawn a tiny pink flower in the middle of her forehead where her third eye should be. Normally she might have sported a few drops of fake blood, or perhaps a tiny skull and crossbones.

"Yeah, I guess I am," Ramona said. "Dan has to stay late tomorrow to help us lay out the next issue of *Inchworm*. So I thought I'd make brownies for everyone tonight. You know, to make layout more fun. I was going to write 'Thanks Dan' in walnuts on the top."

"Dan's allergic to walnuts." Oops. Lina clapped her mouth shut. She shouldn't have said that. It just slipped out.

"What? How do you know that?" Ramona turned her intense black eyes on Lina and gave her the stare. The stare used to scare Lina, but not anymore. Well, maybe a little.

Lina shrugged and tried to act casual. "I think he said something about it in class once."

"No, he didn't," Ramona said. "I write down every

word that man says in class, and he never once said he was allergic to walnuts. Unless I was out sick that day. In which case Chandra or Siobhan would have filled me in immediately. You know I live for every scrap of personal detail I can get about Dan."

Yes, Lina knew. She tried to steady herself under the force field of the stare. She felt herself starting to shake.

"I would like an answer to my question, Ozu," Ramona said. "How do you know that Dan is allergic to walnuts if he never said it in class?"

"He must have mentioned it some other time, then," Lina said. "Maybe he wrote it on one of my papers. How am I supposed to reme.nber a little thing like that?" She tried to laugh it off, as if it were the silliest thing in the world. But Ramona didn't fall for it.

"You know as well as I do that when it comes to Dan trivia your mind is like a steel trap," Ramona said. "Inside your brain are files documenting every significant fact about Dan, where it came from and when you learned it. You're hiding something from me and I want to know what it is NOW."

Lina was pressed against the back of her chair as Ramona leaned forward, her eyes burrowing into Lina's as if she could dig out the truth that way.

"Tell me, Lina. What's going on? It's something big,

isn't it? You wouldn't be so reluctant to share if it wasn't something HUGE."

Lina realized she hadn't breathed in several minutes. She would never, ever, ever tell Ramona, or anyone, about her plan to meet Dan. But to protect that secret, she was going to have to throw Ramona a bone. And the bone itself was so big and juicy that Lina knew it would satisfy her.

"All right," Lina said. "I'll tell you. But you can't tell anyone else. Not even the Cult. Do you swear?"

"I swear." Ramona spit in her palm, rubbed her index finger in the saliva, and offered it to Lina. "Do you want to do a spit-swapping ceremony? Spit on your finger and rub it on mine."

"That won't be necessary." Lina curled her fingers into her palms just to be safe. "Now promise."

"I promise. Now what is it? It's really good, isn't it. I can tell."

"I think you'll find it interesting. A few weeks ago I was browsing through a Web site that had personal ads on it—"

"Oh my god!" Ramona clapped her hand against her mouth in anticipation.

"—And I found an ad from Dan."

"NO!" Ramona practically screamed. Two women sitting near the fireplace turned their heads.

"Yes. Ramona, it was so amazing. It tells all kinds of

stuff about him that you'd never know otherwise. And when you read it, it makes you like him even more." It was kind of a relief to share this with someone who really got it, finally. Holly and Mads thought it was funny, but Ramona knew it was earth-shattering.

"I'm going to die! I'm going to keel over and croak right here on the floor!"

Lina took a moment to let this sink in. She understood. It was big.

"Can I see it?" Ramona asked. "What site is it on?"

Lina hesitated. If Ramona saw the ad she could answer it, too. And that could ruin everything.

"I might show it to you," Lina said. "But first I have to explain something."

"Oh my god. You wrote to him! Didn't you! You did! You fiend!"

"I wrote to him under another name. I pretended to be a grad student his age, so he wouldn't freak."

"Obviously, because if he knew it was you he'd head for the hills," Ramona said. "So?"

"He wrote back. And we've been writing each other every day since then."

Ramona's face was frozen in a stalled scream. Lina almost wanted to laugh. She had never made such a big impression on another person before.

Finally Ramona pressed her hands on the table and bowed her head three times. "Lina Ozu, you are a goddess. I'm not worthy. I knew you had it in you! Way to plot and scheme!"

"Thanks," Lina said.

"You are my superior in every way," Ramona said. "I can't believe what you've accomplished in such a short time. I'm—I'm flabbergasted. And to look at you—no one would ever guess. I mean, you look so sweet and straight, but you're as devious as the worst of us, aren't you?"

"Well, wait a minute—"

Ramona held up her hand. "No need for modesty. You're with a peer. Listen, you have to come home with me. I want to see that ad. I promise I won't do anything to ruin it for you—I'm way too impressed. But I want to know everything that has happened. And I think it's time you finally sucked it up and came to the museum."

Lina swallowed. She'd been avoiding the Museum of Dan ever since she first heard about it.

"We're going to print out that ad and put it on the altar," Ramona said. "Just you and me. We'll do a sacred love ceremony. And you can stay for dinner if you want. What do you say?"

Lina thought about her upcoming date with Dan. She could use all the help she could get—even supernatural help was better than nothing. And she couldn't put Ramona off forever. Someday she would have to see the museum, queasy as the idea made her feel.

"Please, Lina?" Ramona begged. Lina was knocked off-guard by that—it was not like Ramona to beg. "Please."

"All right," Lina said. "I'll come. Just let me call my mother."

"Hi, Dad," Ramona said to a short, squat man cooking soup in the kitchen. "This is Lina."

The man turned away from the stove and bowed slightly to Lina. He had a round, genial, bald head punctuated by a black mustache. "Hello, Lina. Staying for dinner?"

"Yes, she is," Ramona said. She grabbed Lina by the wrist and led her toward the stairs.

"Hope you like bat wing soup!" Mr. Fernandez called after them.

Lina shot Ramona a look. "Is he kidding?"

"Yes, of course he's kidding," Ramona said. "What did you think, we're really witches or something?"

Well, why not? Lina thought. With the way Ramona dressed and behaved, her preoccupation with the occult and a dad who looked like the father on the *Addams Family*, it wasn't much of a stretch.

"Where's your mother?" Lina asked.

"Still at work, I guess," Ramona said. "She sells real estate. A lot of people like to look at houses after work."

So Ramona's mother was a real estate agent. That burst the gothic image a little bit. Unless her specialty was haunted houses.

"Here it is," Ramona said. Her room was in the attic. She pushed open the door, which had been painted dark red.

It would have been a sweet attic room in a Victorian house, with eaves and a dormer window, except for the black fishnet curtains, the black walls with glow-in-the-dark occult symbols painted on them, and the giant Deathzilla poster on the closet door. Deathzilla was Ramona's favorite heavy-metal band. Their symbol was a giant fire-breathing metal robot-dinosaur.

There were candles, vases of dried flowers, bowls of mysterious objects scattered here and there, books and boots and scarves on the floor, and an antique vanity cluttered with jewelry and makeup. On the bed, though, strangely, was a pretty pink ruffled cover with nothing Goth about it at all.

Ramona had set up the museum in a corner. A giant pentagram had been drawn in the floor in chalk. Inside it were four big cushions, one for each cult member to sit on, all facing an old oriental screen that had been turned into a shrine. A few pictures of Dan clipped from the *Seer* were tacked to the screen, as well as favorite Dan-graded papers. The memorabilia—the cups, the pizza crust, a baggy with stray hairs, a piece of chalk, a chewed pencil—were arranged on a small table in front of it, with a candle and a vase of flowers. It was very modest and kind of touching in a way. The creepy thing was that if you didn't know what this was supposed to be, you'd think Dan was dead.

"This is where the magic happens," Ramona said. "Literally."

"Well, not *literally*," Lina said. "I mean, real magic doesn't happen here, right?"

"Who says?" Ramona looked defensive.

Lina let it drop. Ramona turned on her computer. "I can't wait to see this ad," she said. Lina logged on to The List and found Dan's ad. He hadn't changed it since Lina started writing to him. Ramona drank it in.

"Beauregard," she said. "I wouldn't have picked that name for him. It's so *Gone with the Wind*."

"I think it's kind of courtly and old-fashioned," Lina said.

"I'd call him 'Vladimir,'" Ramona said.

"He's so not a Vladimir."

Ramona bowed deeply. "You'd know better than I would, my Queen."

"Stop bowing at me," Lina snapped. "It makes me nervous."

Ramona bowed again. "Whatever you say, oh She-Poobah of the Cult."

"Quit it!" Why did Ramona have to do things like that? Just when Lina felt ready to relax around her, Ramona did little things that annoyed and alienated her. It was as if she felt compelled not to be too likable.

Ramona printed out the ad. "This will become the focus of the shrine. It's the best piece of memorabilia we've got. The Cult is forever in your debt."

"Ugh. Please."

"Ramona!" A woman's voice called from downstairs. "Dinner in half an hour!"

"Okay!" Ramona called back. "Mom's home. Come on, let's do the ceremony." She picked up a pack of matches, more candles, and some incense. "Grab that cloak, would you?" She indicated a satiny green hooded cape draped over a chair.

Lina picked it up. "Why green?"

"It's all I had. Leftover from Dad's Jolly Green Giant costume a few Halloweens ago."

Ramona lit the candle and set things up. "You sit on

that blue cushion and watch," Ramona said.

Lina sat down. Ramona pinned the printout of Dan's ad to the center of the altar. She knelt on a cushion and bowed before it.

"Daniel Shulman, Daniel Shulman, Daniel Shulman," Ramona chanted. "Namluhs Leinad, Namluhs Leinad, Namluhs Leinad. We call to you from another world, a world without school, where divisions melt away."

Oh, I can't take this, Lina thought. She gripped her cushion to keep herself from running away.

Ramona lit a stick of incense and sprayed herself with some kind of musky cologne. She got to her feet and twirled around three times.

"Let us meet in that better world, free of illusion, more real than this one," Ramona said. She bowed to the stack of used coffee cups. "We bow to that which your lips have touched."

Oh, god, get me out of here, Lina thought.

Ramona bowed to the papers and pencil. "We bow to that which your hands have touched." She bowed to what was left of the pizza crust, now little more than a pile of crumbs. "We bow to that which your teeth have touched. . . . "

Lina cringed. But Ramona was so sincere about this. So heartfelt. What made her go through these rituals every week—or was it every day? Did she really think this was going to work?

Ramona put some powder in a saucer, then took a tiny hair from the baggie and stirred it in. She set a match to the powder and it exploded with a pop. "See the light as it burns, See the truth in the fire, You have but two loves, Ramona and Lina, Ramona and Lina, Ramona and Lina . . ."

Ramona and Lina. Lina wanted to cry out for Ramona to stop. But it would be so rude, mean even.

On the other hand . . . What would Dan think if he could see her now?

" . . . We bow to you, our beloved, and plead with Venus, the goddess of love, to grant us your heart . . ."

He'd think she was some kind of nut. And he'd be right.

18 Beauregard Meets Larissa

To:	linaonme
From:	your daily horoscope

HERE IS TODAY'S HOROSCOPE: CANCER: You'll come to a fork in the road today. Take it.

L ina woke up on Saturday morning with a lump in the pit of her stomach. Today was the day—her date with Dan. There were two possibilities. It could be the happiest day of her life. Or the worst.

She had a plan for getting into the city. She'd bike into town and take a cab to the ferry that crossed the bay and docked in San Francisco. Once she was in the city she could get around by taxi, bus, trolley, or BART, the subway system. She'd withdrawn some money from her savings account the day before to be sure she had enough cash. Everything was set. All she had to do now was give her parents a convincing reason why she was going to be gone all day.

"You know, I miss your bangs," her mother, Sylvia, said by way of greeting when Lina entered the kitchen for breakfast. "And your hair's getting a little too long. We ought to schedule an appointment with Terry soon."

Terry was her mother's hairdresser. Lina didn't see why she needed to do anything to her hair—it was long and straight and her bangs had grown out months ago. But she supposed she could use a trim.

"All right, Mom," Lina said. "Maybe next Saturday." She leaned over to kiss her father, Ken, who was reading the paper and eating a bowl of cereal. "Morning, Dad."

"Morning, Lina Lolabrigida," her father said, using an old pet name for her. "I think your hair looks fine."

"Thanks." Lina toasted an English muffin for herself. It was all she could keep down, she was so nervous.

"You excited about this afternoon?" Ken asked.

Lina started. This afternoon? How did he know?

"Um, excited?" she said. "What do you mean?"

"The Forbushes," Sylvia said. She sipped black coffee and ate fruit salad. "I'm sure I mentioned it to you. They're taking us out on their boat today."

"Looks like a perfect day for it too," Ken said. "Sunny, light winds from the southwest—"

The Forbushes! They were friends of her parents with two kids, June and Brendan, near her age. Lina didn't remember anything about going sailing with them today. She knew she'd remember if Sylvia had mentioned it. She glared at Sylvia, who refused to meet her eye.

"You never told me about it," Lina said.

"Yes, I did," Sylvia insisted. "I'm sure I did. I left a note on your desk at the very least."

A note on her desk. That old trick. It could have easily gotten lost—if her mother ever really left it. Sylvia was a doctor, and very busy, and sometimes she forgot things. But she hated to admit it. She couldn't stand to be wrong, ever.

"I never saw any note," Lina said. She looked to Ken for support.

"Sorry, honey," he said. "I should have said something."

"Well, I can't go," Lina said, and in a panic tried to come up with an excuse. It had to be better than the one she'd planned—a day of shopping with Holly and Mads—because that one wouldn't fly. They'd only tell her to cancel it.

"Lina, the Forbushes are looking forward to seeing you," Sylvia said in that way she had, implying that she would make Lina suffer for disappointing the Forbushes long after the Forbushes themselves had forgotten all about it.

"But there's a big girls' soccer match today," Lina said, hoping that was true, in case Sylvia decided to check. "And I've got to cover it for the paper."

"When will we see your first byline?" Ken asked. Lina had decided against showing them her journalistic debut, "Badminton Smackdown," for obvious reasons. Luckily, she had a swim team story coming up next week. A real one, not a made-up one about Sean.

"Soon," she said.

"My daughter the sportswriter," Ken said. "I love it."

"She takes after you more every day," Sylvia said in another typical tone of voice, where it was hard to tell whether taking after her dad was a good thing or a bad thing. What Lina loved about her dad was that he always chose to hear the good thing in his wife's voice, and not the bad. In that respect, Lina *didn't* take after him.

"Anyway, Lina, you're just going to have to find someone to fill in for you," Sylvia said. "We've been planning this day with the Forbushes for weeks."

"She can't do that!" Ken said. "What kind of journalist would she be if she skipped a story to go sailing?"

"Thanks, Dad," Lina said. "It's an away game, in Durban, so I'll be gone all afternoon." Durban was a town about forty-five minutes away.

"Do you need a ride?" Ken asked.

"I'll catch a ride with the team," Lina said. Her muffin was ready. She buttered it, spread orange marmalade on it, and took it to her room with a glass of juice. She thought she'd better get out of the kitchen as fast as she could—before Sylvia found a hole in her story.

The trip into the city was surprisingly easy. *I ought to do this more often*, Lina thought. She walked down a busy downtown street, looking for The Garden Restaurant.

She had agonized over what to wear, wavering between play-it-cool jeans and a glamorous, grown-up silk dress, but finally decided on a pretty flowered dress and sweater.

Here it was. The Garden Restaurant. The doorway was draped with vines. Perfect.

She took a deep breath. This was it. Do or die, now or never, put up or shut up, all that stuff. She hadn't eaten a thing since the English muffin she'd had for breakfast and she was glad, because she would have thrown up from nervousness otherwise. She could feel the blood rush through her veins. She opened the door.

She was greeted by a blast of oompah music. She glanced around the restaurant in shock and dismay. A woman in a traditional German peasant outfit, white blouse and embroidered apron-like dress pushing up her bosom, hair in braids twisted on top of her head, stopped her. "*Guten tag!* Can I help you?"

Guten tag? Was that German? What was this place?

A chubby waiter in green lederhosen and a matching felt hat swept past, a platter of sausages and sauerkraut balanced on one shoulder. The band, a tuba, a trombone, and a bass drum, *oomp*ed and *pah*ed. Big tables full of drunken tourists laughed and clapped. The walls were decorated with Christmas lights and scenes of the Bavarian woods.

Oh my god, Lina thought. It's a German beer garden. The hokiest German beer garden this side of Disneyland. It's noisy, it's kitschy, and it's the least romantic place in the whole city of San Francisco. What would Dan think? It was not very Larissa. Unless she meant it ironically . . . well, that was the only explanation. Larissa would have to be an ironic hipster now.

She glanced around the low-ceilinged, wood-beamed room. No sign of Dan. Just a lot of stout, red-faced people clanking big steins of beer together and bursting into song. "Roll out the barrel, we'll have a barrel of fun . . ." Lina tried to steady herself. Her nerves couldn't take this.

"May I help you, Fraulein?" the hostess asked again.

"Yes," Lina said. "I mean, no. I'm meeting someone. I don't see him yet."

"Maybe he's outside in the garden," the hostess suggested.

The garden. Maybe it wouldn't be so bad out there. Lina threaded her way through the dining room and stopped at the threshold of a small courtyard. A vine-covered trellis made a canopy against the sky. It was a beautiful day, so the courtyard was full of lunchtime revelers, too. And in the corner, at a table for two, sat Dan.

Lina's heart pounded. He was waiting for her. Her destiny sat precariously balanced in that moment. What would happen when she approached his table? He'd be surprised, for sure. But then what? Happy? Upset? Hurt by her deception? Secretly thrilled? Would he pull out a chair and offer her a seat, or would he storm out in an angry huff?

If he welcomed her, she'd be ecstatic. But if he rejected her, she couldn't bear it. Lina looked into her heart, forced herself to be as honest as she could, and weighed the probabilities. The chance of rejection was high. Maybe too high to risk.

He hadn't seen her yet. There was still time to back out. She lingered on the garden threshold a moment longer—a moment too long. He turned his head, looking for the waiter, and spotted her.

Her breath caught in her throat. He recognized her, smiled, and waved.

Oh my god, Lina thought. *He doesn't look upset. Maybe everything is going to be okay.*

She crossed the patio to his table. The oompah band followed her into the garden. Great.

"Hey, Lina," he said. "What a funny coincidence. What are you doing here?"

He has no idea, Lina realized. That Lina could be Larissa seemed so impossible to him that it hadn't crossed his mind. He thought this was just a coincidence.

I'm Larissa! she wanted to say. *Don't you get it? You're waiting for me. I set this up, that's what I'm doing here.*

She opened her mouth. "Well," she began, "I—"

Oom, pah, boom boom smash! The oompah band had followed her and blasted a new song. People in the garden sang along. *"In heaven there is no beer, that's why we drink it here . . . "*

"What did you say?" Dan shouted.

"I'm—" She hesitated. Should she say it? *I'm Larissa.* It wasn't that hard. What was stopping her?

"I'm—" She couldn't tell him. It wasn't right, the way she'd tricked him into writing her and falling for her. She could get him into a lot of trouble—and he was completely innocent. So innocent that he'd never guess in a million years what she'd done.

"And when we're gone from here, all our friends will be drinking all the beer!"

Thank god for the oompah band, Lina thought. It had saved her. But now she needed a believable reason why she'd traveled miles from home just to come to a cheesy place like this. There was a blissful pause in the music. "I'm in the city shopping with a friend," Lina told Dan. "I just ducked in here to use the bathroom."

Dan nodded. "I'm supposed to meet someone here. She chose this place. I have to admit it makes me wonder about her."

Lina felt terrible. Dan didn't know it yet, but Larissa would never show up. He'd be stuck in that beer garden for a long time, tortured by the oompah band, waiting for her. Poor Dan.

"Well, I'd better go," she said, a little sadly. "See you at school."

"Nice to see you, Lina. Have a fun day in the city."

"Thanks." She walked back to the dining room, stopping one last time at the threshold of the garden. Dan had pulled a paperback from his pocket and started reading. At least he had something to keep him busy.

She sighed, and mentally blew him a kiss. Then she went home.

19 Karaoke Kritic

| To: | hollygolitely |
| From: | your daily horoscope |

HERE IS TODAY'S HOROSCOPE: CAPRICORN: How low can you go? Pretty darn low.

So what did you do this afternoon?" Holly asked Lina. It was 7:30 Saturday night and they were sitting at a small table in Room 1 of Kay's Karaoke Palace, watching Autumn, whose birthday it was, butcher "Your Song" by Elton John. Autumn's beloved, Vince, sat in front of her, beaming adoringly. Mads was due to arrive any minute with that guy Stephen she was always yammering about.

"Um, I went sailing," Lina said. "With my parents and

some friends of theirs." She sipped her strawberry smoothie, which came decorated with a paper umbrella in a glass the size of a fish bowl.

"Cool," Holly said. "Nice day for a sail. I helped Eugenia search the pockets of all Dad's suits for signs he's having an affair. An uplifting way to spend a Saturday."

"Did you find anything?" Lina asked.

"Depends," Holly said. "Does a pink golf tee count? Because that's all we found. Jen says the fact that it's pink proves he was golfing with a woman, which he doesn't usually do."

"I think Jen's reaching a little here," Lina said.

"Me, too. I really don't think Curt's having an affair. I think he just doesn't like being around Jen that much lately. Which is just as bad. Maybe worse."

Mads arrived with Stephen in tow. He looked a little uncomfortable, checking out the other kids. This wasn't his usual crowd.

"Did we miss anything good?" Mads asked. They crammed themselves around the table, Stephen between Holly and Mads.

"Hi, Holly," Stephen said.

"Hi," Holly said. "You didn't miss much. Just love songs, nothing but love songs, from the birthday girl."

"I've never met the famous Autumn," Stephen said.

"There she is," Mads said. Autumn still hogged the microphone, crooning "Endless Love" with Vince. "The famous Autumn. Famous for good reason. You should have seen the invitation to her party." Mads described it to him.

Autumn Nelson's Karaoke Party
Kay's Karaoke Palace
Saturday night from 7 till ???
Here's what your life will be like if you don't come to my karaoke party—Loserville! Everyone will be talking about all the cool things that happened and you will have missed it! Your life will be over! So if you want a reason to keep on living, come to my party!

"Was it an invitation or a threat?" Stephen asked.

"Exactly," Mads said.

"Vince did a knockout Sinatra impression. I never would have guessed," Lina said.

"Oh, and Rob and Christie are competing with Autumn and Vince for first prize in the Couples Who Make You Want to Throw Up Contest," Holly added.

Rob and Christie were only two tables away. "Endless Love," in spite of its name, finally ended, and they could hear Christie fussing and cooing over Rob.

"You look so cute in that shirt, Sweetie-Pants," Christie said. "It shows off your big swimmer-boy muscles."

Rob was wearing yet another of his t-shirts, GUNS DON'T KILL PEOPLE—POSTAL WORKERS DO. Holly put her finger in her mouth and made a gagging noise.

"They're not really that big," Rob said, staring at his upper arm. "But thanks. You look nice, too. I like that barrette you're wearing, Chris." She was wearing a huge, hideous cow-shaped barrette in her hair. He had his arms around her, and she kissed him between sentences.

"Honey-pie," Christie corrected. "Remember, you're supposed to call me 'Honey-pie.'"

"Right. Sorry, Honey-pie. Hey—mind if I kiss you, Honey-pie?"

"I love the way you ask me that," Christie said. They kissed again.

"You guys might not want to sit with me," Holly said. "Because the chance of precipitation is 100 percent. I'll either be puking or crying, one or the other." Clearly Rob was in no danger of being criticized for anything by Christie. And no one would ever call her picky. And she obviously didn't mind constant PDA.

"Number 2507!" Rebecca called out. Partygoers passed around black vinyl notebooks filled with song titles. Each song had a number next to it. You picked out the song you wanted to sing, wrote down the title and number on a slip of paper, and turned it in to the guy who worked the karaoke machine. When your number came up, it was your turn to sing.

"That's me," Rob said. He got up and walked to the stage.

"This should be interesting," Holly said. "I've never heard him sing before."

The music started. The title flashed on the screen. "God Save the Queen" by the Sex Pistols.

"Oh no, not a punk song," Holly groaned. "That's karaoke suicide."

The song started. Rob tried to rasp it out. Really badly. He stank. But it was okay because he knew he stank and he didn't care, he was just having a good time. Holly liked that about him. Still, he stank.

Everyone clapped when he was done—they were all friends, after all. He returned to his table and Christie.

"You were so great!" she gushed. "You sounded just like Johnny Rotten. You totally rocked the house!"

"Thanks," Rob said. "I know I can't really sing, but—"

"You can so totally sing!" Christie said. "You should go on *American Idol*. I'm serious."

"That puke-fest you talked about, Holly," Mads whispered. "Can anyone join?"

"The worst part is, he's eating it up!" Holly said. "He loves it." But the real worst part was she still wanted him back. What would she have to do to get him? Was Christie really the kind of girl he wanted?

All right, Rob Safran, Holly thought. *I see what's going on here. You like a girl who loves everything about you. A girl who will never criticize you. Well, I can do that. If that's the kind of girl you want, that's what I'll be.*

The old Holly would have made a crack about the postal worker shirt. But the new Holly keeps her mouth shut. If she doesn't have something nice to say, she says nothing at all. Maybe she'd even broadcast the message to Rob through song. She flipped through the songbook, looking for "Just the Way You Are."

"So—that guy used to be your boyfriend?" Stephen asked Holly.

Mads stepped in before Holly could answer. "They went out a few times, but she's totally over him now."

Stephen nodded and glanced back at Rob. Holly threw Mads a look but didn't say anything. What was going on? Mads knew that wasn't true.

The party was in full swing now. It was hard to hear people talk, what with all the cheesy belting going on. Lina spotted Walker at a table with a few of his friends. He waved to her. Autumn flounced over to Holly's table and pulled up a chair.

"Thanks for coming to my party," she said. "I knew

you wouldn't want to miss it. Hey—did you hear about Alex Sipress's party Friday night? It's going to rock!"

Holly glanced at Mads. This was a sore subject for her.

"Is everybody going to Alex's?" Mads asked. "I'm having a party that night, too, you know."

"Oh yeah, that's right," Autumn said. "But Alex's parents will be out of town. Plus he's a senior. So I think his party wins. Sorry, Madison. Why don't you have your party another night?"

"Because I already invited everybody and it's supposed to be an Art Fair party!" Mads said.

"Well, I'm sure some people will still show up," Autumn said.

"Number 4707!" Rebecca called.

"Oh! That's me again." Autumn hurried to the stage to sing "Yesterday."

"I might as well just cancel my party," Mads said. "It's going to be a complete flop."

"We'll still come, Mads," Lina said.

"Me, too," Stephen said. "I don't care that Alex Whoever's parents will be out of town."

"Thanks, guys," Mads said. "But Alex's will be more fun."

"Don't cancel it," Holly said. "You don't know what's going to happen. Maybe your party will be a big hit! Wait and see."

"I can't cancel it, anyway," Mads said. "My parents and my aunt and uncle will be there. Even if no one else shows up, I have to go. God, I can't believe I have to go to my own lame party! I wish I could blow it off."

"You know what you need?" Stephen said. "A song." He paged through the songbook and wrote down a number. "When they call 3416, go up on stage."

"What song is it?" Mads said. "What if I don't know it?"

"You know it," Stephen said. He gave the number to the karaoke guy.

"Girls, I haven't seen any of you up there yet," Sebastiano said, pulling up a chair.

"Number 3416!" Rebecca shouted.

"That's you, Mads!" Lina said.

"Oh no," Mads said.

"Get up there!" Sebastiano dragged her to her feet and pushed her toward the stage. The song title came up. "Satisfaction" by the Rolling Stones.

"That's a tough one," Holly said. "No one but Mick Jagger can do it right."

"She knows it by heart," Stephen said. "I heard her singing it under her breath one day while she was drawing. She gets this little growl in her voice . . . I'm telling you, she can do it."

Mads started singing, shyly at first, but before long

she was growling and shouting and strutting across the tiny stage. Soon the crowd was on her side, singing along during the chorus. When it was over the whole room roared. People slapped Mads' hands as she went back to her table in a daze.

"Wow, that was fun!" she said.

"Way to work that crowd, Mads," Sebastiano said. "You've got hidden star power."

"You think so?"

"Well, it's a really catchy song," Sebastiano said.

Walker came over. "Lina, I've got a song coming up soon and I need a partner."

Lina shrank back. The last thing she felt like doing was getting on stage and singing. She was still recovering from her secret rendezvous that afternoon. And going from oompah band to karaoke—it was a little too much kitsch for one day.

"Sorry, Walker, I can't," she said. "I'm kind of tired—"

He grabbed her hand and pulled her out of her seat. "Too bad. This is a duet. I'm not singing it alone. You want me to look like an idiot?"

"No," Lina said. "But I don't want to look like an idiot, either."

"Come on, Lina," Holly said. "Everybody has to go up at least once."

"It's fun!" Mads said.

Lina could see she had no choice. Walker's song came up, an oldie called "Don't Go Breaking My Heart" by Elton John and Kiki Dee.

"Do you know it?" Walker asked.

Lina nodded. "My dad likes to listen to the seventies station."

"My mom, too. She used to sing this one to me."

They started out shyly, but soon picked up speed. Lina looked at the audience, just kids from school, her friends, swaying and clapping along. She let herself go and before she knew it, the song was over.

"Awesome! Wooo!" the crowd cheered. Lina stumbled through the clapping crowd back to her table.

"You rock!" Mads said.

"You were right, it was fun," Lina said.

Holly couldn't quite forget that Rob and Christie were there, but she was starting to have a good time at least. Then the number was called for another duet—this time, Rob and Christie.

Sebastiano looked at Holly expectantly. "I'm waiting," he said. "Snarky remark? When's it coming?"

"It's not," Holly said. "This is the new, non-critical Holly. No snarky remarks. Christie seems like a very nice girl."

"Please, Holly," Sebastiano said. "If you can last five

minutes without insulting her, I'll be shocked."

Rob and Christie sang "Crazy in Love" by Beyonce and Jay-Z. It sucked. Christie was a worse singer than Rob. But, fatally, she lacked his sense of humor about it. She seemed to think she was Jessica Simpson up there, dancing and singing her little heart out.

"Ouch," Sebastiano said, trying to goad Holly. "We're talking first-round *American Idol* reject."

"She's doing her best," Holly said. "What more can we ask?"

"Come on, Holly. Look at the way she dances! Like a bee just stung her butt! You know you want to say it."

"That would only be petty of me," Holly said. "Christie's probably a good person inside. Isn't that what counts?"

"Holly, now you're the one who's making me sick," Mads said.

"Shh! Don't worry, Mads," Sebastiano said. "She's going to crack any minute now."

"No, I won't," Holly insisted. "You must think I have no self-control at all."

No one said a word.

"Thanks a lot," Holly said.

The duet ended. Unfortunately, it threw a bit of a pall over the party.

"You know what, Holly? You're right," Sebastiano

said. "It really wasn't so bad. It was like outsider art. You know that art that prisoners and mental patients make out of junk? It's very popular these days."

"Yeah," Holly said. "Except even a mental patient wouldn't wear a giant barrette in the shape of a cow."

Whoops.

"Aha!" Sebastiano cried. "Got you!"

She couldn't help it. It was so hard not to be catty when Sebastiano was around. "It just slipped out," Holly said. "It's all your fault!" And right when Rob was passing her table. She looked up. Yes, he definitely heard her.

"You know what your problem is, Holly?" Rob said. "You're so busy criticizing everyone else that you don't know how to have fun. I haven't seen you get up and sing yet. I'll bet you're afraid to. Maybe somebody in the audience will be as mean and critical as you are."

He went back to his table. Christie giggled and covered her mouth.

"Whoa," Sebastiano said. "He got you good."

Holly sighed and slumped in her seat. "That's ridiculous," she said. "He's wrong. I know how to have fun. I'm not afraid."

But true or not, it didn't matter. If that was what Rob thought of her, she'd never get him back.

20 Off to India

To: linaonme
From: your daily horoscope

HERE IS TODAY'S HOROSCOPE: CANCER: Your stars show a lot of lying and sneaking around—they've actually taken the shape of a tangled web. I can't condone this. Just what the heck is going on out there?

To: Larissa
From: Beauregard
Re: ???
Dear Larissa,
I guess you know what I'm about to ask you. Maybe I shouldn't ask, but I have to know—why didn't you show up today? Did I get the address wrong? The date? The

time? I went to The Garden Restaurant at five to one and waited for you for three hours. I would have stayed longer but if I had to listen to that band play "Roll Out the Barrel" one more time I was going to shoot someone. Probably myself. (An odd choice of meeting place, I might add—but that only deepens your mystery for me. What kind of girl would go to a place like that? An unusual girl, to say the least. Unless, of course, you never planned on showing up at all and only wanted to torture me.)

And so, if you could give me the dignity of an explanation, I would appreciate it. If you would like me to stop writing, I will. If I don't hear from you, you won't hear from me again. Forgive my somber tone, but you can't imagine how much I was looking forward to meeting you—and how disappointed and disillusioned I was when you never came.

—Beauregard

Lina found Dan's e-mail waiting for her when she got home from Autumn's party. It broke her heart to read it. She felt ashamed, and his scolding tone only made things worse. What could she say? What kind of excuse could she give for the terrible way she had treated him? And how could she get out of meeting him face-to-face without losing this precious correspondence?

Because she knew she couldn't meet him, not like this. He was too tied up with Larissa, emotionally. Finding out Larissa was one of his students might upset him even more than never knowing who she was at all.

But at the same time, she couldn't let go of Beauregard. He meant too much to her. His e-mails made her feel warm inside, beautiful and loved. And being Larissa was so much fun! Larissa felt almost real to Lina—a real part of her, the grown-up Lina who hadn't emerged yet, but would some day.

She took a deep breath and tried to think straight. Her hands were shaking. All right. She had to make up some reason why she couldn't meet him, something believable, something he could forgive.

To: Beauregard
From: Larissa
Re: I'm so sorry!
Dear Beau,
I'm so sorry I didn't get to meet you today, but I have a good
    excuse, I swear! I just got back from the animal hospi-
    tal. I was leaving to meet you when my cat suddenly got
    very sick—he swallowed a whole bag of gummi worms.
    Turns out they're like poison for cats—they get stuck in

their guts. The vet rushed him into surgery and he just
came out. Looks like he'll be okay. I would have called
but I had no way to reach you. I'm so sorry. I didn't think
you'd wait for me so long.

The Garden is a funny place, isn't it? I know it's cheesy, but I
thought we could meet there, have a laugh, and then
go someplace nicer. I can't believe you had to suffer
with that band for three hours! You must have ears of
steel.

Well, I'd better go to bed—I'm very tired. It's been a long day,
and I have to get up early to visit Spike at the hospital. I
hope you'll forgive me.

—Lara

She sent the e-mail, and a few minutes later a reply
came. Dan must have been sitting up, waiting to hear
from her.

To: Larissa
From: Beauregard
Re: I'm so sorry!
Lara—
I'm sorry to hear about your cat. I hope he'll be all right. I had
no idea gummi worms were so toxic. Did you name your
cat after a filmmaker—Spike Jonze, maybe, or Spike

Lee? And I forgive you. I hope you forgive me for my
angry e-mail and for not understanding immediately that
you must have had a good excuse not to show up.
So let's make another date. When can we meet again? Next
weekend, perhaps? Only anywhere but the Garden, if
you don't mind.
Greatly relieved,
Beau

Hmm—she should have checked with Mads' mother
before going out on a limb with that toxic gummi worm
thing. It probably wasn't true. This problem wasn't going
to go away, was it? He still wanted to meet her. She had
to come up with some reason why he could never meet
her, at least not for the next few years. But what?

This would be a true test of Lina's writing and lying
skills.

To: Beauregard
From: Larissa
Re: Off to India
Dear Beau,
I wish I could meet you. I'd love to meet you. Believe me, I'm
so curious about you I could burst! But there's one
problem. A big problem. I just found out I was accepted

at the Bollywood Film Center in Mumbai, India. I'm going
there to study the techniques of the great Indian
filmmakers. My master's thesis is on Indian movies, so
this is crucial for me, as well as a big honor. And
unfortunately, I'm leaving this Saturday. I have so much
to do to get ready, I'm afraid I won't have time to meet
you. There isn't much point anyway, since I'll be away in
India indefinitely. But we can still write, and when I get
back maybe we can get together.

You can keep writing me at this address—my e-mail server
will bounce all my mail to my address in India. And hey,
if you happen to be in India, let me know. Maybe we'll
have our first meeting at the Taj Mahal.

—Larissa

That ought to hold him, Lina thought sadly. She almost
hoped he wouldn't write back. She was going to have to
do a ton of research on India to make it sound as if she
were studying there. Maybe she should have picked Japan
instead—at least her ancestors came from there. But that
was so long ago—the 1880s—that even her grandmother
didn't know much about it.

Dan didn't write back that night. Maybe he was
digesting what she'd written, trying to figure out what was
real and what was a lie. She hoped he didn't come too

close to the truth, which was that it was all lies. No truth in any of the e-mails she'd ever sent him. Except for this one fact: She had a big crush on him. And now she liked him more than ever. She'd just have to find another way to make him hers.

21 True Love vs. Artistic Integrity

HERE IS TODAY'S HOROSCOPE: VIRGO: Nothing you do turns out the way you planned—thank goodness. If you ran the universe it would be a huge mess.

Mads stepped away from her easel and stared at the big poster-sized pastel drawing of Sean she had made. The pose was the same as in the digital photo she'd taken of him. But blown up so large—four feet tall—the picture made a very different impression. Sean stood on the tile in his bathing suit, goggles around his neck, rubber cap in one hand, arms outstretched, flexing his biceps. The muscles bulged slightly.

The look on his face was, well, how would Mads put it? Confident was probably the nicest way of saying it. Smug would be less charitable. Vain would come closest to the truth.

"Stephen, come here," Mads called. Stephen had finished his installation, but he wouldn't let anyone, including Mads, see the final product. He had taken it apart and was packing it away to move into the gym in the morning, where he'd set it up before the Art Fair began.

"What's up?" Stephen asked. "All done?" He crossed the room to look at her work.

"All done," Mads said. "What do you think?"

Stephen crossed his arms and stared at the picture. Mads watched his face. His mouth twisted in an odd way. Then it bunched up toward his nose. He looked as if he were about to sneeze. He covered his face with his hands.

"What?" Mads asked. "What is it?"

Stephen let his hands fall from his face. He burst out laughing.

"It's hilarious!" he said. "It's really good, Mads. It captures him perfectly." He collapsed on the floor in a fit of laughter.

"What's so funny?" Mads asked. "Why are you—" She turned to the picture, and it hit her. She'd worked so hard to show how gorgeous Sean was, and he did look gorgeous—but it was almost too much. The picture was like a cartoon of a Greek statue—and the expression on his face said he took himself completely seriously. The contrast between the self-satisfied look on his face and the goofy Hercules pose . . . Stephen was still laughing. Mads started laughing, too.

"Oh—my—god—" Mads struggled to speak through her laughter. "You're right. It's—so—funny—"

She sank to the floor and they leaned against each other, back to back, clutching their stomachs and laughing. Mads' head accidentally clonked against his. "Ow!" they cried at the same time, and laughed even harder, rubbing their sore heads.

Mads had worked hard on that picture. She'd been so serious about it. But the look on Sean's face—

Stephen caught his breath. "I hope you don't take this the wrong way, Mads. It's a good picture. Really good. The best one of your portraits. Except maybe the picture of Holly. That one's great, too."

Of course—she knew he loved that one.

"The way you suggest the atmosphere of the pool behind him is brilliant," he said. "And that pose—" They were overtaken by another round of giggles. "If only Sean could see it . . ."

Mads stopped laughing. Oh no! Sean *was* going to

see it. The very next day. She started to get nervous.

What would he think? He'd probably hate it—and be angry with Mads for making fun of him. Furious! He might never speak to her again!

"Maybe I should keep it out of the fair," Mads said.

"What?" Stephen was indignant. "You can't. It's a great drawing, Mads. Bet you win a prize."

"But—"

"If you withdraw that picture from the fair, I'll personally put it back in. I'll take credit for it if I have to. People need to see that picture. Sean more than anybody."

Mads looked at the picture again. She knew it was good. She wanted to win a prize. Maybe Sean would be cool about it. But it would probably piss Sean off.

"Maybe the Holly picture will win a prize," she said.

"Maybe," Stephen said. She watched him admire it. He stared at the portrait of Holly for a long time.

He really likes Holly, Mads thought. *If Holly would just pay attention to him. . . .* She was supposed to meet Holly and Lina at Vineland in half an hour. Maybe she should bring Stephen along and see what kind of trouble she could stir up.

"Are you almost finished packing up your stuff?" she asked Stephen. "Want to go get some coffee with me?"

Stephen looked surprised and pleased. *Wait till he sees*

Holly, she thought. *Then he'll be really happy.* "Sounds good. I'll be ready in a few minutes."

Mads pulled open the door to the café and spotted Holly and Lina waiting at a table.

"So—is this kind of like a date?" Stephen asked.

Mads looked at him, surprised. Did he know what she was up to, now that he saw Holly?

"I guess it's not exactly a date," Mads said. "It's just coffee. But a date could be arranged, if you're interested."

"I'd like that," Stephen said.

Okay, so now it was out in the open. Stephen wanted her to fix him up with Holly. All she had to do was get Holly to agree—which might not be so easy. But maybe they'd hit it off this afternoon.

Holly and Lina were already on their second lattes. Stephen smiled shyly at them.

"Hey, guys," Holly said. "All ready for the big art show?"

"You should see Mads' portraits," Stephen said. "They're so good."

"I heard your installation is awesome, too," Holly said. "Mads told us about it. What she saw of it."

"She hasn't seen it all together yet," Stephen said. "No one has. I want it to be a surprise, for ultimate impact."

"How are the party plans coming, Mads?" Lina asked.

"Okay, I guess," Mads said. "It shouldn't be a total disaster, as long as my parents don't ruin everything."

"Can I invite Ramona?" Lina asked. "I mean, if you don't have too many people coming."

Mads snorted. "Are you kidding? Too many people? That won't be a problem. But I thought you didn't like Ramona."

Lina wasn't sure how to explain. "I do and I don't," she said. "We have a weird relationship. But I know she'd like to come."

"Invite her then," Mads said.

"I need to ask a favor, too," Holly said. "Can I bring Britta Fowler to your party?"

"Who's Britta Fowler?" Mads asked.

"She's a junior," Holly said. "Her parents are friends with Curt and Jen. She's a really nice girl, but she studies all the time and she's never had a boyfriend. She's my next matchmaking challenge. I figure if I could match Autumn successfully, I can match anybody. And anyway, her parents asked me to help boost her social life a little."

"Bring her," Mads said. "I hope she doesn't mind sucky parties. Because my party is going to suck. Everybody else will be at Alex's."

"It won't suck, Mads," Holly said. "But Britta won't

know the difference anyway."

"Don't worry, Mads," Stephen said. "All the *really* cool people will be there." He looked from Mads to Lina to Holly. Mads thought his eyes lingered on Holly an extra second. Holly smiled at him. Jackpot!

As they were leaving, Stephen said to Mads, "You have nice friends."

"Thanks," Mads said. "They like you too."

"I'm glad," Stephen said.

Everything was fine on the Stephen side. If she could just get Holly to give him a chance.

I'll talk to her tomorrow, Mads said to herself. *I'll ask her to go out with Stephen, and if she resists I'll talk her into it. Then everyone will be happy.*

Except for Sean, when he sees his picture.

And me, after Sean sees his picture and hates me. And after my party bombs and my popularity level plummets to its lowest point ever.

Oh well. Being semi-coolish was nice while it lasted.

22 The Art Fair

A rt students were excused from classes Friday morning to set up their displays in the Salon des Arts, otherwise known as the gym. Frank Welling allotted Mads three temporary pasteboard panels. She carefully pinned up her pastel portraits—M.C., the Overlord, Audrey, and Adam on the left wall; Holly, Lina, her boxer puppy Boris, and Captain Meow-Meow on the right wall; and in the center, pride of place, her masterpiece, the largest of her portraits and the only full-length one, *The Swimmer.*

"Maybe Sean won't notice it," Mads said to Ramona, who had stopped by to say she would be happy to attend Mads' post-fair party. Ramona had her own entry in the fair, just one drawing, a pen-and-ink called, *Souvenirs of My Latest Trip to Hell.* "He might not recognize himself. I didn't put his name on the picture."

"Hate to break it to you, but there's no chance of that," Ramona said. "Unless he doesn't come to the fair at all."

"That's possible," Mads said. "Sean's not a huge rah-rah school guy."

"Everybody takes at least one stroll through the Art Fair," Ramona said. "Somebody will tell him about it. Every art fair has one piece good for a laugh or a shock. This year, looks like you're it."

Great. Mads wanted to be the talk of the fair, but not because she'd pissed off the most popular guy in school.

"It's really good, though," Ramona added. "See you later."

Mads peered around the maze of temporary display walls and spotted Stephen in a back corner, putting up his installation. The "walls" of the "bedroom" were covered with paper, to be unveiled only once the show opened. He waved to her and called, "Stay away! No peeking until showtime!"

"Okay, then same goes for you," she said. "You can't see my stuff until show time either."

"I've already seen all your stuff," Stephen said. "You didn't chicken out, did you?"

Mads knew he was talking about the Sean portrait. "No," Mads said. "It's up."

He gave her a thumbs-up and went back to work. She watched him a few minutes longer. Something about him, his seriousness or industriousness, appealed to her. Was that a tiny crushy feeling tickling her inside? She immediately repressed it. Holly needed a distraction from Rob; she needed Stephen more. And anyway, Stephen liked Holly, not Mads. It wasn't meant to be.

At lunch time the fair officially opened and the students began to stream in. The judges, mostly art teachers from other schools, walked slowly through the maze, studying each piece carefully and making notes. Holly and Lina made a beeline for Mads' display.

"Awesome!" Holly cried. "Sean looks like he's ready to dive right out of the picture."

"Congratulations, Mads," Lina said. "Your pictures are beautiful."

"Have you seen Christie Hubbard's stuff yet?" Holly asked.

"No," Mads said. "I haven't had a chance to walk

around the rest of the Fair. Is it any good?"

"I haven't seen it, either," Holly said. She bit her lip. Rob was still bothering her, Mads could tell.

"Holly, listen," Mads said. "You need to stop thinking about Rob. I know someone who really likes you, and I think you'd like him, too."

"Who?" Holly looked wary.

"Stephen," Mads said. "I know he'd go out with you if you wanted to. He thinks you're the most beautiful girl in school. And he's very nice. And he never wears t-shirts with funny slogans on them. Should I fix you guys up?"

"He thinks I'm beautiful? How do you know?"

"He said so," Mads told her. "When he saw your portrait, he told me he thought it was gorgeous."

"It is gorgeous," Lina said.

Holly thought it over for a minute. "He seems like a good guy," she said. "But I don't want to go out with him, Mads. I'm still hung up on Rob."

Mads was exasperated. "But what about Christie? Isn't she kind of, you know, in the way?"

"I'm about to take care of that," Holly said. "I'm going to look at her paintings or drawings or play-doh sculpture or whatever right now. And no matter how bad it is, I'm going to praise it to the skies, right in front of Rob. Then he'll see how nice I can be. I am not picky and I'm not critical—and

I'm going to make Rob see it if I have to get down on my knees and bow before his stupid moron of a girlfriend."

"I hope he finds the new uncritical Holly more believable than I do," Lina said. "If he knows you at all, I don't think he'll fall for it. Am I right, Mads?"

Mads didn't answer. She kept thinking about Stephen. She had practically promised him a date with Holly, and now Holly wouldn't go. How was she going to break it to him?

Mads wanted to get away from her own display and look around, but she never had a chance. She was stuck in her spot all afternoon. People kept coming by, asking her questions about her pictures and telling her how good they were. The judges stopped and looked, smiled and nodded and scribbled things in their notebooks. Sean's picture was a big hit. Some of Sean's friends, Alex, Mo, and Barton, stopped at Mads' booth, stared, and cracked up.

"Dude, check out Benedetto!" Barton said.

"Wait until he sees this," Mo said. "Muscle man in his swimsuit. And the look on his face. That's his Superstud face."

"Hey, kid," Alex said. "Awesome job. You captured Sean perfectly—right down to his freaky toenail."

It was true. In her typically obsessive way, Mads had noticed Sean's strange, bumpy big toenail. It was ridged and white. You could see it in the photo she took of him, so she carefully copied it onto her drawing.

"You're the Leonardo diCaprio of Rosewood," Alex added.

Mads assumed he meant Leonardo da Vinci and took it as a compliment.

She was glad Sean's friends liked her portrait of him—but the way they were already teasing him about it worried her. *He'll never forgive me,* she thought. *I've sacrificed the love of my life for artistic integrity. I'm such an idiot! It's so not worth it.*

"Let's go see that bedroom thing," Mo said. "Some kid supposedly recreated a whole guy's room. I heard it's really cool."

Late in the afternoon, as the crowd reached critical mass, Sean finally arrived at the fair, alone. He nodded at Mads and said "Hey." Nothing else. He stood in front of the temporary wall. He cast a cursory glance at the portraits of Mads' family and friends. Then he gazed at his own image for a long time. Mads chewed her thumbnail. She knew he'd hate her forever. Maybe he'd never speak to her again. Maybe he'd yell at her. She just wished he'd get it over with.

Finally, he turned to her. She braced herself.

"You know," he said, "I've got a great body."

That knocked the wind out of her. It wasn't what she expected him to say.

"Uh, yeah, you do," she said.

"Cool," he said. "I like the way you drew the muscle tone in my legs."

Her breath returned. The muscle tone in his legs? Was that a compliment for her—or for himself?

"So—you like it?" she asked.

"Hell yeah," Sean said. "Who wouldn't? I mean, I don't like to brag, but I look totally hot in a bathing suit."

"Yeah—exactly!" Mads said. "You do look hot in a bathing suit. Which is why I wanted to draw you that way. I'm so glad you like it!"

"'Course I like it, kid. You can draw me anytime."

Frank Welling and the judges reappeared, ribbons in their hands. "That's the one," one of the judges said. She pressed a blue ribbon next to the portrait of Sean. "Madison Markowitz, you get first prize for portraiture. Nice work."

"Good job, Madison," Frank said. "Especially for a sophomore."

"See, kid, I told you it was good," Sean said.

"Thank you!" Mads said. She won a blue ribbon!

She'd hardly dared to hope for one. But she'd won. And it was all thanks to Sean.

"Hey, Sean," Mads said. "You know, I'm having a party at my house tonight. To celebrate my prize-winning portrait of you. It's a party in your honor in a way, so you have to be there. You'll come, right?"

"How can I miss a party in honor of me?" Sean said. "Sure, I'll be there. And I'll make all my deadbeat friends come, too."

"But what about Alex's party?" Mads couldn't stop herself from asking. She didn't want Sean to promise to come to her party and then not show up.

"No problem—we'll all go after your party. It's a late-night thing anyway," Sean said. "You should come, too. Ditch your party after a couple of hours and come with me over to Alex's."

"You're inviting me?"

"Sure, I'm inviting you. You're like my portrait-painter chick. Maybe you'll want to draw more pictures of me. You've got to have access to your subject."

"Thanks!" Mads was thrilled. Sean invited her to Alex's party! And he was coming to hers! To her house! With her parents . . . oh no. She'd have to make sure her parents and Audrey didn't embarrass her. And Adam and Aunt Georgia and Uncle Skip. They always found a way.

Maybe she could lock them all in a closet or something.

It was turning out to be a great day. Not only did Sean not hate her portrait—he loved it! And he'd invited her to a party, and her party would be cool now. And she'd won a blue ribbon. True love and artistic integrity at the same time. Who said you couldn't have both?

The fair traffic finally slowed down. Mads left her booth and headed for Stephen's installation. Everyone at the fair was buzzing about how cool it was. She was dying to see it, but she dreaded facing Stephen. She'd have to break it to him that he wouldn't be going on a date with Holly anytime soon, if ever.

The installation was big, almost the size of a real room, with three walls, a window, a bed, a closet, a rug—everything. Near the bed a TV monitor flashed videos. A sign next to the installation read THE BOY MAKES THE MAN BY STEPHEN COSTELLO. And next to it was a blue ribbon—First Prize for Best in Show.

"Hey! I won a blue ribbon too!" Mads said.

"Congratulations," Stephen said. "Let me give you the tour." Mads stepped inside the "room" and looked around. It was crammed with stuff to look at, but Mads' eye was drawn to a poster on the wall. It was a pinup style poster of a girl, a teen princess posing in a cute blue dress under the heading THE DREAM GIRL. It almost looked like a movie ad, except the girl in the poster was no movie star—she was Mads!

"Aah!" Mads gasped. "That's me!"

"I know," Stephen said. "You were my model for the ideal girl."

"Me? I was your model?" Mads was stunned. What did this mean? Was it a joke? Was he teasing her? Did she look ridiculous, like Sean in his picture? Mads studied the poster carefully. She didn't think she looked ridiculous. She thought she looked kind of pretty. But then, that's what Sean thought about his picture, too. "You're making fun of me, right?"

"No," Stephen said. "I wanted to show the perfect girl, the kind of girl boys dream about."

"Okay, now I know you're kidding," Mads said. "I'm not the perfect girl. Nobody dreams about me."

"Are you sure?" Stephen asked.

"Well, there is this kid named Gilbert, but he's not normal."

"Do you think I'm normal?" Stephen asked.

What was he trying to say? "Um, I guess so," she said, not sure what he wanted to hear. "I mean, you're not like most boys. But I don't think you're weird or abnormal or anything."

"That's good to know."

Mads felt confused. She was all ready to tell him that Holly didn't want to go out with him, but now she wondered if Holly was the one he liked after all.

"So how about that date?" Stephen asked. "Is it still on?"

"Not exactly," Mads said. "Stephen, I have to tell you something. I hope you won't be too disappointed, but Holly—well, she's still hung up on Rob, and—"

"Holly?" Stephen said. "What does she have to do with it?"

"Isn't she the one you wanted to go out with?" Mads said. "I promised you I'd fix you up with her."

"With Holly? I thought we were talking about you!"

"Me?" Mads was stunned. "But—Holly's picture—"

"It's beautiful," Stephen said. "You did such a good job on it."

"I—?"

"I was admiring the picture, not the subject. I mean, of course Holly's a pretty girl. But what really got me was they way you saw her. Your artistic vision of her."

"My artistic—" Mads' head was reeling.

Stephen led Mads to one of his cardboard chairs and let her sit. It was surprisingly sturdy. "Mads," he said. "You're the one I like. I thought you knew that."

"No," Mads said. "I thought you liked Holly. Most guys like Holly."

"But I like you."

This is too much, Mads thought. *First I win a blue ribbon, then Sean says he'll bring all his friends to cool up my party, then he invites me to Alex's, and then Stephen calls me the ideal girl! And he wants to go out with me!*

"So will you go out with me? Tomorrow night, maybe?" Stephen asked.

Mads wanted to say yes. She pictured herself on a date with Stephen. She hadn't allowed herself to think of him that way before. But now . . . her—and Stephen. Stephen kissing her! She tilted her face toward him. She wished she could kiss him now.

But something stopped her. Sean. Sean had just asked her to Alex's party. Was it a date? What if Sean wanted to go out with her now? What should she do?

She tried to speak, but no words came out. Torn between two lovers! She'd never understood before why that would be a problem, but now she got it.

"You weren't expecting this, were you?" Stephen said. "I caught you off guard. It's okay, Mads, you don't have to answer me right now. Think about it."

"Thanks, Stephen." God, he was so nice. And he liked her! It was going to take a little time to sink in. She never thought a boy like Stephen—a serious, philosophical, artistic boy—would like her. Not in a million years. But he did.

And why not? she thought. She was an artist herself. A blue ribbon artist.

She liked him, too. She'd always liked him. But now all the crushy feelings she'd had for him began to bubble up to the surface. In her mind she repeated the same thrilling sentence, *Stephen likes me! Stephen likes me!*

Still, Sean was there first. And she couldn't pass up a chance with Sean—not after all this time.

23 The Fabulous Party

To:	hollygolitely
From:	your daily horoscope

HERE IS TODAY'S HOROSCOPE: CAPRICORN: Don't go over-board. You want to attack your enemy with an atomic bomb when the flick of a finger is all you need to win. Chill!

Welcome to my fabulous party!" Audrey had staked out the front door dressed in a pink terrycloth minidress and platform sandals, a big blue flower in her strawberry-blond hair.

"Hey there, Malibu Stacy," Holly said. She was one of the first to arrive at Mads' party, and she'd brought a tall girl with small, silver wire-rimmed glasses and lots of curly brown hair. Britta Fowler.

"Audrey, it's not your party!" Mads snapped. "Go out back and help Adam subdue Boris." Boris, the Markowitzes' boxer puppy, kept jumping all over the guests, leaving them covered with muddy paw prints. So far, luckily, only Aunt Georgia and M.C. had been hit, but Mads wasn't about to let Boris destroy her party, so she begged Adam to tie him up.

"I don't want to get all muddy!" Audrey whined.

"Just go away then," Mads said.

"Mads, this is Britta," Holly said, nodding at her friend.

Mads tried to put on a calm hostess smile, even though she was frazzled. "Nice to meet you, Britta. Come on out back—that's where the party is."

Lina, Ramona, Walker, and Sebastiano were already there, sipping drinks out of plastic cups and making polite chitchat with the Overlord and Uncle Skip. It was terrible. Nobody ever had fun at a party where they had to talk to parents all night.

"Turn up the music," Holly advised. "Then your parents can't hear what anyone's saying."

"Brilliant," Mads said. She hurried inside and cranked up the volume. When she returned to the backyard, she found Stephen waiting for her.

"Hi," he said. "Funky house." Mads' house had been built out of cedar in the seventies, and most of the rooms had several different levels. It was hard to tell how many floors the house had.

"Thanks." Mads wanted to take his hand, but she stopped herself. She felt awkward. Sean hadn't arrived yet. But when he did . . . well, she wasn't sure how much time she'd have to talk to Stephen. And he wasn't really friends with anyone else at the party. She led him to the picnic table where Holly, Britta, Lina, Ramona, and Sebastiano sat and listened to Adam holding forth on photosynthesis.

Autumn, Rebecca, and company arrived, and Mads spotted some juniors and seniors she didn't really know. Sean must have spread the word. Soon the backyard was crowded with kids munching on quesadillas, sipping virgin mojitos, and yammering over the music.

Sean arrived with his usual entourage of Mo, Barton, Jen, and Alex. Audrey rushed over to him.

"You're Sean, right? I heard all about you."

Mads raced to her side for damage control. "Hi, Sean. Audrey, M.C. wants you."

"Who's the little chick?" Sean asked, nodding at Audrey. Audrey beamed.

"That's my sister," Mads said. "She was just leaving."

"I'm not going anywhere," Audrey said. She looked Alex up and down. "What's your name?"

"The Boogie Man." Alex made a monster face.

Audrey pouted. "Don't talk down to me just because I'm eleven."

"Whoa. Sor-ry."

"Audrey—" Mads said. "Why don't you all get something to drink?"

Mo, Alex, and Jen filed past her. Pulling up the rear was a tall, leggy blonde in jeans. Jane—the girl Sean had been hanging with for weeks now. It wasn't clear what their relationship was. But Sean grabbed her by the hand, pulled her toward him, and wrapped his arm around her.

Oh. Maybe Mads had misunderstood. Maybe Sean hadn't asked her to Alex's party as a date, but just as part of the group.

A wave of disappointment washed through her. For a few seconds she couldn't move. Sean didn't want her, not yet.

But as the disappointment melted away, she realized she never really believed it was a date. She'd only wished for it.

It's all right, she told herself. *It's still a step in the right direction.* Being part of Sean's group was very cool, and Mads decided that for now, she'd take it.

She glanced across the yard at Stephen, who was talking to Sebastiano. Now she was free to go out with him, and who knew where it would lead? That helped blunt the disappointment, too.

"Jane, you know Madison, right?" Sean said. It was the first time he'd ever bothered to introduce Mads to Jane—or even call her Madison instead of "kid." "She's the girl who drew my prize-winning portrait."

"Hi," Jane said. "Congratulations. *She's* the one who won the prize, you know," she said to Sean. "Not you."

"I'm her model," Sean said. "I deserve a little credit, don't I?"

"You inspired me to new creative heights," Mads said.

"See?" Sean said to Jane. She kissed him. Well. It wasn't the evening Mads was expecting. But now Sean knew her name. And he had come to her house. She was moving ever closer to her goal. In the meantime, she had someone else to keep her busy.

Stephen and Sebastiano were leaning against the lemon tree, laughing over something. Stephen caught her eye and watched her weave toward him through the crowd. The closer she got, the happier Mads felt. She had something good to tell him.

"Hi," she said to Stephen and Sebastiano.

"Great party, Mads," Sebastiano said. "Your little sister's a riot. Do you think she'll sing 'Oops I Did It Again' if I pay her?"

"She'll probably do it for free," Mads said.

"Far out. But I've got gum, just in case she requires a bribe. Does she like Dentyne Ice?" Mads nodded and Sebastiano set out to find Audrey.

"I forgot to ask you," Stephen said. "What did Sean say when he saw the portrait?"

"He said, 'I've got a great body,'" Mads told him.

"Really?" Stephen laughed.

"Um, Stephen?" Mads said. She felt nervous all of a sudden. What if he'd changed his mind? Three hours had passed since he said he liked her. Anything could change in three hours.

"Stephen, would you like to go out tomorrow night?"

"Are you sure?" Stephen said. He looked at the knot of people gathered at the food table. Mads knew he was wondering about Sean.

"Yes, I'm sure," Mads said. "I'm glad you like me, because I like you, too."

"We'll celebrate our blue ribbons," Stephen said. "And our likability."

"I liked you from the beginning, even though you thought my drawing of a cat was a monkey," Mads said.

"You promised to answer a question for me that day, remember?" Stephen said.

Mads remembered. His mother called him St. Stephen the Serious, and Stephen wanted to know if the name fit.

"I wouldn't call you St. Stephen," she said. "You are serious, but you're funny, too. You're good, but I bet you're no saint."

She found herself drawing closer to him without knowing how it happened. She wasn't aware of moving her feet. She was pulled as if by tractor beam.

"You're right," he said. "I'm not a saint. And I'll prove it to you right now."

He bent down to her beaming face and kissed her. Mads got lost in that kiss. She forgot that she was standing in her backyard in plain sight her parents, Aunt Georgia, Uncle Skip, and all her friends.

Stephen straightened up and looked at the crowd behind her. "Whoops. Is that your mother?"

Mads turned around and flushed bright red. M.C. stared at her, a carrot stick frozen halfway to her open mouth. Uncle Skip snapped his fingers in front of M.C.'s face.

"Is she going to be okay?" Stephen asked.

"She'll get over it," Mads said.

Stephen took her hand. "Come on," he said. "Introduce me to her. Mothers usually like me."

Mads caught people glancing at them as they walked hand-in-hand through the party. Lina and Holly looked surprised but happy. Even Sean cast a look her way. He nodded at Stephen and said, "Way to go, dude."

• • •

Lina thought she'd better rescue Ramona, who'd been cornered by Aunt Georgia. Georgia was grilling Ramona on her makeup techniques. She wasn't wearing any make-up herself, but now that she was approaching fifty she was thinking she should start. "I always liked that crazy-lady look for old ladies," Georgia said.

"Me, too." Ramona nodded vigorously. "Lots of white powder, till the face is like a blank sheet of paper. Then draw your features on anyway you want. Those pointy black eyebrows and lots of lip liner. Like a silent film star, or a clown. And blue hair—really blue hair."

"Exactly," Georgia said. "I figure, if I'm going to get old, I might as well make a statement."

"Totally," Ramona agreed. "Like those aging Hollywood actresses. They're the coolest."

Lina stood listening in bewilderment. This was a conversation she could not contribute to.

A bell rang in the kitchen. "That's another batch of quesadillas," Georgia said. "I'll be right back." She hurried into the house.

"What's the news from Beauregard?" Ramona asked.

"Not much," Lina said. "The e-mails have started slowing down." Since Larissa had told Beauregard that she was moving to India, he'd seemed to withdraw. Lina couldn't blame him. Especially after she'd stood him up, sick cat or not.

"Did he say anything about a new job?" Ramona asked.

"No," Lina said. For once Ramona knew something she didn't. "Why?"

"Well, I was sitting outside Alvarado's office yesterday and I overheard his secretary say she heard a rumor that Dan was offered a job at another school next year."

Lina's heart nearly stopped. "No! Where?"

"Don't know," Ramona said.

"Is he moving away?"

Ramona shrugged. "I guess."

"So he's leaving?"

"It's just a rumor. So far."

But a believable rumor. Dan had made it clear to Larissa he wasn't happy with his job at RSAGE. Still, Lina was stunned. Somehow she'd thought he'd always be around—ready and waiting by the time she graduated.

"You know what this means, don't you?" Ramona said. "It's now or never. If one of us is going to make a move, we have to do it now. Before he slips away for good."

For good. Lina couldn't believe she'd just passed up a chance to sit and have lunch with him alone. After this school year she might never see him again. When she was finally old enough to be with him, he will have forgotten all about her.

"We have to do something," Ramona said. "Something more effective than casting spells on him."

"I know," Lina said. But what?

"Look," Ramona said. "This is an emergency. No more secrets. Promise? The two of us have to work together from now on. Is it a deal?"

Lina saw the emotion on Ramona's face. Loving Dan was a kind of loneliness. It was like believing in something no one else could see. But Lina and Ramona had each other, and it would help.

"Yes," Lina said. "The two of us together. It's a deal."

"See anybody cute?" Holly asked Britta. If she was going to make a match for Britta, she needed to know what type of guy she liked.

"He's cute," Britta said, pointing out Rob. "But he's clearly taken."

Rob was wearing a t-shirt that said OLD UPHOLSTERERS NEVER DIE—THEY ALWAYS RECOVER. Holly shuddered. Not so much because of the t-shirt, but because he was sitting on the picnic table with Christie, who was feeding him a quesadilla. She was wearing a t-shirt, too. Hers said

SUPPORT YOUR LOCAL UNDERTAKER—DROP DEAD!

It was bad enough that they never took their hands off each other. Now they were dressing alike, too? Holly thought she was going to be sick.

"Who's the melonhead?" Britta asked.

"Her name is Christie," Holly said. "Rob's dating her."

"That's Rob?" Britta said. "Your Rob?"

Holly nodded.

Britta watched while Christie fed Rob another bite of quesadilla. She kissed him between every bite. At first he seemed to like it. But by the fifth kiss he pulled back and said, "Christie, I haven't had a chance to swallow yet."

Ha, Holly thought. She remembered the way Rob used to kiss her constantly and how it annoyed her sometimes.

Christie straightened up in a huff. But then she handed Rob his drink and wrapped her arms around him, cooing.

"This is so repulsive," Britta said.

"I know," Holly said. "They're always all over each other like that."

Rob tried to put his drink down on the picnic table, but it was hard with Christie holding him so tight. "Christie," he said, "could you let go for one second? I want to set my cup down."

"You didn't say 'pretty please, honey pie.'" Christie kissed him on the ear, then on the cheek.

"Pretty please, honey pie," Rob said. Holly could hear the irritation in his voice. Hmm, this was getting interesting.

Christie released him. He stood up and stretched. Then she put her arm around him and stuck it in his back pocket.

"There's Laura," Christie said, pointing out one of her friends. "Let's go talk to her."

"I'll catch up with you later," Rob said. "I'm going to see what Walker's up to."

"No," Christie said. "Stay with me. Come on, Robby-bobby."

Rob took her hand out of his pocket. "Christie, it won't kill you to spend ten minutes talking to your friends without me. We haven't been surgically attached—yet."

Whoa. Look at Rob—standing up for himself!

"About time he said something," Britta said.

Christie gaped at him in surprise. "My friends were right about you!" she squeaked. "You're not affectionate enough! You might as well be made of metal! You don't love me!"

She ran across the yard to her friend Laura. Rob watched her, looking baffled.

"This is so weird," Holly said to Britta. "I dumped him partly because he was too affectionate. He likes to kiss every five minutes. I can't believe it's not enough for her!"

Rob shook his head and sat down on the bench. Then he spotted Holly. He gave her a little smile and a wave.

Look at him, she thought. So cute. She didn't care about his silly t-shirts—those had nothing to do with the warm person he was inside. And he didn't *have* to wear them—it wasn't as if they were tattooed on his chest. Anyway, he'd probably grow out of them soon.

"Go over to him," Britta said. "He wants you to."

Holly was nervous. After all, the last time she'd confronted him he said he didn't want her back. And it had crushed her. But he was worth risking another try. She walked over and sat beside him on the picnic table.

"You know what, Holly?" he said. "I think I understand how you felt when we were together. Like we had a little too much of a good thing?"

"But it *was* a good thing," Holly said. "I hate your t-shirt, by the way."

Rob laughed. "It's one of my favorites. But I don't have to wear them all the time. I'm getting a little tired of them. Christie really likes them."

"Really? She seems like such a paragon of taste."

"I can't take her anymore," Rob said. "No matter how nice I am to her, it's never enough."

"She's crazy," Holly said. "You're the sweetest, most affectionate guy I know."

Rob gazed into her eyes. He still liked her—she could feel it. He always did have a thing for her eyes.

"Christie's always demanding more," he said. "But I never had that problem with you. You never took advantage of me and you always told me how you felt."

"But I was too picky," Holly said. "All those little things that bugged me were so silly. What I really care about is the real you—the guy who knows how to make me feel better when I'm sad. The guy who makes happy times happier. . ."

She kissed him. He put his arms around her.

"I want my Holly back," he murmured. "The Anti-Christie."

A scream emanated from across the yard. The crowd parted as Christie raced over to Rob and Holly.

"What are you doing?" Christie shrieked. "Why are you kissing her?"

"Christie, I'm sorry—" Rob began.

"You're horrible!" Christie cried. She picked up a handful of tortilla chips and pelted him with them. That didn't have much impact, so she gave up and dumped the whole bowl on his head. Then she ran away in tears.

Holly took the bowl off Rob's head and helped him

brush the chips off. The party went quiet.

"Well," Holly said. "That was awkward."

"I didn't want to upset her like that," Rob said. "I probably should have found a nicer way to break up with her."

"She started it," Holly said. "She accused you of being made of metal."

Mads and Lina came running over. "Is everything okay?" Mads asked. "What happened to Christie?"

Rob put his arm around Holly, and she leaned against him, feeling happy. People started talking again, the music blared, and the party went back to normal.

"Hey," Lina said. "Are you two back together?"

Holly glanced at Rob. "Yes," he said. "We're back."

"Yay! Rob and Holly are back!" Mads cheered.

"We always thought you guys should be together," Lina said.

"It was just a temporary setback," Rob said.

"Hey, Mads," Holly said. "I just thought of another quiz topic. 'Was Your Party a Hit or a Flop?'"

"I like it," Mads said.

"Give yourself a point for every time you answer yes to one of these questions," Holly said. "Question One: Were the coolest kids in school there?"

"Yes," Mads said.

"Question Two: Did any new couples get together?" Holly asked.

"Yes," Lina said. "Mads and Stephen!"

Mads grinned and waved at Stephen, who was stuck talking to her father. "The Overlord loves him already."

"Question Three: Did the neighbors complain about the noise?" Holly asked.

Mads beamed. "Yes! We already got an angry call from the Zieglers."

"Question Four: Was there a fight?" Holly said. "Did at least one person leave in tears?"

"Yes and yes," Mads said.

"Well, Mads," Holly said, "looks like your party is a big hit!"

"And it's not even over yet," Mads said. "Maybe the police will come! People would talk about that for weeks."

"We can only hope," Holly said.

Can True Love Survive High School?

Lina jumped on her bike and pedaled toward the water. Carlton Bay was a waterfront town, full of boat piers and seafood restaurants and a weathered boardwalk that ran along the shore called the Marina. Ramona was waiting for her on a bench, licking an ice cream cone, her own bike leaning against a rail.

"Heard you got an eyeful at the game today," Ramona said. Drops of pink ice cream dripped into her raven hair and down her ragged black dress and tights. *She really has the Goth look down,* Lina thought, taking in Ramona's black outfit, green nails, and elaborate mask of Goth makeup. Around her neck Ramona wore a thin orange tie, a symbol of her love for Dan, their teacher, who always wore skinny ties.

"I can't believe how fast word gets around when there's nudity involved," Lina said. A streaker had run onto the field at the varsity lacrosse game.

"Sit down, we've got to talk fast," Ramona said. "I don't have that much time. My mom's having trouble unloading a house, and she wants me to put a spell on the buyers."

Ramona was into spells and voodoo. Her mother was a real estate agent, not Goth at all, but it looked like Ramona was drawing her into her web. Lina would have thought real estate was immune to supernatural power, but obviously she was wrong.

"First of all," Ramona said, "I surrender him to you."

"What?" Ramona was nearly as in love with Dan as Lina was, and very competitive. It wasn't like her to surrender anything to anyone.

"Look, there's no time to fool around," Ramona said. "Only one of us can have him, right? I mean, if you look at it realistically. And that's what we've got to do—be realistic. So, you're the one who's been secretly e-mailing him and all. Once we get him, he's yours. I just want to live vicariously through you. But you have to promise to tell me every detail, no matter how personal or gross. Promise?"

"I promise."

"Really? Do you swear? Do I have to extract some kind of elaborate vow from you?"

"No, you can trust me, Ramona. You know that."

"I do *not* know that, but I don't have much choice. Now. How are we going to get him?"

Lina thought a minute. "Um, what are we talking about, exactly? What do you mean, get him?"

"Well, you know . . ." Ramona trailed off. That was the thing about loving a teacher. You longed, you yearned, but for what exactly? It was so unlikely you'd get anywhere with him that you didn't have to think that far ahead.

"You're going to be his girlfriend," Ramona finally announced.

And that was what Lina wanted. But somehow she found it hard to picture.

"We'll start slow," Ramona said. "Let's say our goal is that by the end of the month he will think of you as different from the other students. Special."

Secretly, Lina hoped he already felt this way. "That's not enough."

"Okay. The two of you have to be somewhere alone together. Not school-related. And it has to be understood that what you're doing is not a student-teacher thing, but a guy-girl thing."

Ramona was rolling now. "I've got it. We'll send him a note from 'a secret admirer' and get him to meet us somewhere. You'll go up to him with a black veil over your face, so he can't see who you are, and then—"

"Ramona—" Lina elbowed her in the ribs. A familiar figure was walking toward them down the boardwalk.

"What? I'm on a roll here. Then, when the moment is right, you rip off the veil—"

"Ramona! Look!" Lina nodded at the man, who was coming closer. It was him. Dan.

Ramona clutched Lina's arm. "Oh my god! It's him! I conjured him with my psychic brain waves! I knew I had powers!"

"Ow—Ramona, your claws are digging into my skin." Lina peeled Ramona's hand off her arm.

"This is a sign," Ramona whispered. "This is our moment. We've got to act NOW!"

"Now? What are we going to do?"

"Just go!" Ramona yanked Lina to her feet. Dan had nearly reached them.

"Ramona, stop it!" Lina whispered. "I thought you had to go home and cast a spell on some real estate."

"That can wait."

"At least tell me what the plan is!"